Control # 930 35478

$18 $\underline{00}$

W9-BLZ-778

HANNAH IN BETWEEN

by

Colby Rodowsky

Troll Medallion

Copyright © 1994 by Colby Rodowsky.

Published by Troll Medallion, an imprint and trademark of Troll Communications L.L.C.

This edition is reprinted by arrangement with Farrar, Straus & Giroux.

Printed in the United States of America.

10   9   8   7   6   5   4   3   2   1

Lyrics from "So Long (It's Been Good To Know Yuh)" by Woody Guthrie © 1950 (renewed) and 1963 (renewed) Folkways Music Publishers, Inc., New York, New York. Used by permission.

Library of Congress Cataloging-in-Publication Data

Rodowsky, Colby F.
    Hannah in between / Colby Rodowsky.—1st ed.
    p.   cm.
    ISBN 0-8167-3740-1 (pbk.)
    [1. Alcoholism—Fiction.   2. Family problems—Fiction.
    3. Mothers and daughters—Fiction.]   I. Title.
    PZ7.R6185Han   1994   [Fic]—dc20   93-35478   CIP   AC

For Will and his sister Ellen

HANNAH
IN
BETWEEN

One

"Take a deep breath, Hannah, and blow the candles out," Granddad said. Then he stopped and waited a minute before going on and saying exactly what I knew he'd say, what he says every year. "How many is it this year—twelve?"

"That's right, Granddad—twelve," I said.

"Twelve—*wow*," he said, same as he had said "Eleven—*wow*" last year and "Ten—*wow*" the year before that. I can just imagine him standing there next to me and my first birthday cake, saying, "Well, there, Hannah-banana. And today you're one. *Wow*."

That's the thing about my grandfather. He's predictable. But in a nice way. Being with him is sort of like wearing a broken-down pair of sneakers or listening to a favorite song over and over again. Comfortable, too.

In fact, up till now if I'd had to choose two words that described my life, I'd've picked *predictable* and *comfortable*. Predictable because of the way we almost always get pizza on Friday nights and Granddad makes blueberry pancakes after Sunday church and my best friend Sam (who's really Samantha) and I talk on the phone for hours sometimes and Dad and Mom and I like to go for walks to places we've never been. Comfortable, I guess, because I like the way it's so predictable. Maybe, now that I think about it, it should all be one word: *precomfordictable*.

Probably the most precomfordictable part of my life has always been the summer part, the beach part. Pretty much, I guess, because it *is* summer and vacation and most of the people I see year round (except for Sam) are there and have more time. Anyway, it's like this: for years, forever, since before I was born, Granddad and Gloria (who's his second wife and not my real grandmother because she died before I was born, but who's really neat anyway and as good as a real grandmother) have had this house at the shore, set, sort of, in the midst of the piney woods and across the bay from Ocean City. And every summer Mom and Dad (who's Granddad's son, to keep things straight) and I go there for a month and stay in a rented house just down the road. Same as Aunt Pauli and Uncle Bill (who's also Granddad's son) and their son, Casey, stay in another rented house.

And every year, once we're there we do the same

precomfordictable summer things: we swim and walk and ride bikes and go crabbing and play about a hundred million games of Monopoly. We talk and sit on porches and just let the days roll over us. Mom takes pictures (she's a photographer) and Dad reads a lot and tries to think up new and different things to do when school opens in September (he's an English teacher in high school) and I mostly hang out with my friends, with Mandy and Sue and Jessie Lee, who I've known since we first started coming here and who I only see in summer because after that they go back to Virginia and Pennsylvania and Delaware. And I stay in Maryland— but go back to Baltimore.

And the most predictable thing of the summer is my birthday. It's August 29, and we celebrate it every year, on Granddad and Gloria's porch just at dusk and before the mosquitoes are out. Celebrate it with cake and ice cream and my favorite mints, the kind with licorice inside, and with coffee for the grownups. And with presents for me.

Except a lot of things have changed. Because of my mother and how she drinks too much. Because of how she's gone from being a regular mom who did regular things like sitting on the foot of my bed and talking every night before I went to sleep, trying on big floppy hats in stores, and buying me paperback books for no occasion to someone who spills her drinks and has head-aches a lot and sometimes forgets to do what she said she would.

The thing is, I'm not sure exactly when it started. I mean, it's like watching the grass grow. No one actually *sees* it grow. It just *does*.

Another thing: because no one ever *says* anything about this, I think maybe I'm the only one who knows what's going on.

And scariest of all is that what's happening with Mom has changed me, too: how I act with Dad and Sam and everybody else.

"Come on, Hannah, blow. Where are you—on another planet or something?" said Mandy, moving close and jabbing me with her elbow. "We're hungry."

"Yeah, blow," said Sue.

"Before the candles all melt and there's nothing left but wax soup," said Jessie Lee.

"You heard your friends, Hannah-banana. Now go ahead and blow—I've got a date and have to get out of here," said Casey, sitting on the porch rail and kicking his feet against the slats. Casey's in college and good-looking in a Kevin Costner but younger kind of way. He's nice, too, and sometimes I pretend he's my brother and not my cousin. That's the thing about me—I pretend a lot. And make up stuff. But that's okay because if I do decide to become a writer when I grow up, which I'm seriously thinking of doing, then none of it will've been wasted but will be just so much grist for the mill. That's what Granddad says: all of life is grist for the writer's mill. And he ought to know because he's a writer, and kind of a famous one.

"Blow, Hannah," said Mom, her voice sounding thick and shadowed. "Blow, blow, blow."

I did and the candles went out all in a swoosh and then it was dark and quiet for a minute before everybody started singing "Happy Birthday to You." Weird, but that's the way we do it in our family: sing after the candles are out.

"Did you make a wish?" asked Mom, rolling the ice cubes around in her glass. "What was it?" She leaned forward and caught me by the wrist so that the skin felt all pinched and twisted and I wasn't sure what to do, 'cause everybody knows you can't tell your wish. No matter what.

"Oh, no, she can't do that—it won't come true," Aunt Pauli said in that quick way she has of saying what everybody else is already thinking. Then she jumped up and hurried around serving ice cream in bowls, while Gloria cut the cake.

"So, Granddad, did you write your column yet?" asked Casey, reaching for a piece of cake.

"Which column would that be?" said Granddad, and we all laughed. Even me, except with me it sort of hurt some, the way it does when you have to laugh but you'd rather not be doing it. That's because the column they all had in mind was about *me*—Hannah Jane Brant.

It's like this: Granddad had two sons, and his first grandchild, Casey, was a boy, too, so that when I finally came along he was so glad to have a girl in the family, as Gloria tells it, that he wrote a column about it. And he kept on writing them—every year on the day after my birthday (because he wrote the first one the day *after* I was born), there I am in a headline: "Hannah at One," "Hannah at Two," right on up to where I am now.

And the trouble is, he tells things, about me, I mean.

Like the year when I was two and I learned to say "Santa Claus, ho-ho-ho," and how other years I took ballet and chased butterflies and learned to ride a bike, got my ears pierced, and wrote my first poem. It was all there, my whole entire life spread out—and not just in the Baltimore paper but also in the other papers Granddad's syndicated in. That's because, as I said before, he's sort of famous and the rest of the time he writes about politics and stuff. One thing, though: the Hannah columns make me feel shy and embarrassed and I've never mentioned them to Granddad. He never talks about them to me either, so maybe he feels the same way.

"Okay, you all, this is a party and a party means presents," said Gloria, getting up to clear the table. Then everybody was piling packages in front of me and I was sitting there acting cool and like I wasn't just itching to tear into them.

"Present time," my mother sort of sang out. She stood up and swayed over the table. "Present time . . . present time . . . present time . . ."

I tried to ignore her and to concentrate, instead, on a small square box at the top of the heap that just *had* to be the pair of scrimshaw earrings I'd been looking at in the window of the Sea Shell all summer long.

"Present time," my mother said again, and out of the corner of my eye I saw my father reach for her and touch her on the arm. She pulled away from him and headed inside, bouncing against the doorframe as she went, and in a minute I heard her moving around the kitchen.

"Open mine first," said Jessie Lee.

"Open anything," said Casey. "I've got to get moving."

"Here," said Aunt Pauli, handing me something big and squishy wrapped in newspaper. "It's from Casey."

I tore at the paper and took out a bright red sweatshirt with UNIVERSITY OF MARYLAND across the front in white letters. "Oh, great, thanks, Casey," I said as I put it on, rubbing at the sleeves and liking the way they felt soft and warm against my bare arms. "Now everybody'll think I'm in college."

"Come on, Hannah, you're on a roll. Let's keep going here," said Dad. And I did, opening up a Walkman and the scrimshaw earrings, two tapes and a poster, and, at the very end, a book of Emily Dickinson's poems from Gloria and Granddad. But all the while, through the laughter and the funny remarks, what I mostly could hear was the sound of my mother lurching around the kitchen and the clatter of ice cubes that sounded louder than all the rest of us put together.

When the party was over, Mandy, Sue, Jessie Lee, and I went down to the bay and onto the pier, spreading out beach towels and lounge chairs. Moonbathing, we called it, and we'd been doing it ever since we were little and discovered that if we went somewhere and were quiet at night, our parents forgot about us and let us stay up really late. Mostly we watched for skimmers and falling stars and listened to the night sounds all around us. Sometimes we told ghost stories, and this year we made up a romance, adding to it for seventeen nights. It was good, too, and we thought we would sell it to a soap opera company, except that by the time we got to the end we'd forgotten the beginning. We're going to do another one next year—and write it down.

Tonight, though, we pretty much talked about what we'd done during the summer and what we were going to do next year in school and how maybe *this* winter the four of us'd actually get together at somebody's house for a weekend. We knew we probably wouldn't, though, because just getting home from the beach makes it all seem a million miles away and even when we write letters they aren't very good letters and we're almost like strangers. Until the next year.

"It's kind of sad," said Jessie Lee. "The end of summer, I mean."

"Don't talk about it," said Mandy, who never likes to be sad and doesn't even want to cry at books. "Let's everybody tell what we're going to do tomorrow—for our next-to-last day."

And I rubbed my arms in Casey's big red sweatshirt and said, "I know what I'm doing. I'm going into Ocean City with my mom and we'll pretend we've never been there before and do all kinds of touristy things: go to the beach and ride the waves and eat Italian ices and spend the whole afternoon. And maybe we'll even get telescope pictures taken."

"You're not going to do something with us?" asked Mandy. "You're not coming to the pool?"

"I might, maybe in the morning before we go," I said. "But anyway, remember how we're going to the boardwalk at night. We'll be together then. But this is something Mom and I've wanted to do all month. Something she promised me."

"You know what I'm going to do?" said Sue. "Sleep late and go to the pool and eat lunch there and—"

"Till your mother grabs you and says you have to pack," said Mandy.

"Till all our mothers grab us," said Jessie Lee.

There was a crashing noise in the underbrush leading down to the beach, like it was a bear, except there aren't any bears in Ocean Pines, and my mother came out onto the sand. "Present time," she sang as she held her glass up to the moonlight. She came over to the end of the pier and stood looking out at us. "Present time?" she said again, but this time in the shape of a question.

"No, we had that, Mrs. Brant," said Jessie Lee. "Now we're moonbathing."

"Moonbathing?" said Mom as if she hadn't heard us talk about moonbathing for maybe a hundred years. "Oh." She set her glass on top of a piling and stepped onto the end of the pier and stood there for a minute, sort of teetering. And just then, almost in one big swoop, my father came down the path and out onto the beach. He caught Mom around the shoulder, turning her back toward Granddad's house. "Katherine, I've been looking for you," he said. "We're getting started on a game of Monopoly and we need you."

For a minute Mom didn't move, as if she was thinking about whether she really wanted to play Monopoly or not. Then she reached around and took her glass off the piling and went with my father up the path.

It wasn't till after she was gone that I realized I'd been holding my breath; that my lungs hurt and my throat burned. I sank down lower in my lounge chair and wrapped my arms across my chest, shivering in spite of my sweatshirt.

Jessie Lee started to sing, in that funny squeaky voice of hers. "I see the moon and the moon sees me, the moon sees somebody I want to see."

Then Mandy and Sue joined in. "God bless the moon and God bless me, and God bless somebody I want to see."

And the whole time they were singing, I stared up at that hard yellow moon. Stared at it until my eyes ached.

Two

I woke early the next morning, mostly, I guess, 'cause it was the next-to-last day of vacation and there's something about next-to-last days that makes you grab at them and keep them from being gobbled away too fast. I got up and stood by the window, pulling on shorts and a shirt and thinking how, more than anything, I wanted to go out by myself, to watch the light over the bay. How I wanted to walk through the pine woods, sliding on the fallen needles, and smell the smell that's sharp and sweet and prickly all at the same time.

I eased my bedroom door open, slipping into the hall. The house was quiet with the kind of quiet you notice when you know you're the only one awake, and I moved into the living room, looking at the jumble of newspapers, at Dad's Dock-Sides in front of the television. Then I stopped in the kitchen for a glass of orange juice and went through the sliding glass door and onto the porch.

Taped to the outside of the door was a strip of paper, fluttering there in the breeze, and I knew, before I unstuck it, what it would be. Same as I knew that Gloria had put it there. "Hannah at Twelve," I read as I went over and sat on the step. I smoothed the column against my leg, flattening the edges, and trying to read and not to read both at the same time. "My granddaughter, Hannah, is twelve," Granddad began, the way he begins every year except with a different age. I skipped down to the bottom to see if he'd ended the way I knew he would and read out loud, in a singsongy voice, "Happy birthday, Hannah."

Then I read the in-between part, all about how this was the year I got braces and went to my first boy-girl party and learned to play tennis. And the way he'd written it, anybody would think it was all really terrific. The thing is, though, that Granddad doesn't always exactly tell the truth, and if he'd wanted to write a *real* column he ought to've put in how the braces make me look like a metal mouth, and the party was a disaster with all the boys hanging over Nintendo and the girls standing around acting as if we didn't care. And when I play tennis, it's pretty much like I have a hole in my racket. I mean, I miss a lot.

After that part, Granddad did something really weird, even for him. He talked about my name, how Hannah meant "God has favored me," and how I was getting to look like his mother, my great-grandmother, whose name was also Hannah. My skin crawled, just reading it mostly, I guess, 'cause I know I don't look anything like her. In the pictures I'd seen, Great-grandmother Hannah had been pretty and sort of curved—not spindly, with moppy dark hair and about a million mosquito bites. And as for that other part, about God, I mean . . . Well, I wasn't sure. I mean, I know I have a lot of things and compared to most people in the world I'm incredibly lucky—but, even so, sometimes I'm not sure about God *really* favoring *me.* Then I didn't want to think about it anymore, or have Granddad make me think about it, so I rolled the column as tight and small as it would go and shoved it in my pocket.

I went down to the shore and walked along kicking at the water and listening to the hum of speedboats out on the bay. I climbed up onto a fallen tree trunk and stood balancing there for a minute before I followed a trail of footprints around a curve and into a cove.

"Good morning," called Gloria from her place on the beach.

"Morning," I answered, going toward her and thinking how even though I'd started out to be by myself, being with Gloria was almost as good.

"Thanks for the column, I guess," I said, sitting next to her and shoving my feet down into the cold, wet sand and shivering slightly.

"Well, I know how you like to get a chance to read it on your own, and not with everybody looking over your shoulder."

"Yeah," I said. "Only Granddad exaggerates, about my life and all."

"He wants things to be perfect for you, Hannah," said Gloria.

But they're not, I wanted to say. They're not. They're not. And for a minute I felt the same as I do when I'm on the Ferris wheel and about to go over the top and down the other side all in a rush. And for a minute I thought I could tell Gloria about the things that worry me a lot—about Mom and how she is different than she used to be, about the drinking and how maybe I'm the only one who knows it and just thinking about it and carrying the weight of it makes me tired. "But what if I'm wrong?" I asked myself. "What if it's not true?" And I knew I couldn't say anything, not even to Gloria, so I took my secret and shoved it back inside of me same as I shoved my feet deeper into the sand.

"When are you and Granddad going home—to Baltimore, I mean?" I said after a while, when I was sure my voice'd work and sound okay and not like I'd changed my mind about saying something else.

"Oh, after Labor Day," said Gloria. "Once you all pull out, and Bill and Pauli and Casey, too, it gets really quiet around here and we'll be anxious to get to town. Now, what are you doing with your next-to-last day?"

"Going to the beach," I said. "Into Ocean City. Mom said we would, just the two of us. We'll get lunch at the Alaska stand and just sort of hang out, and we might even get a telescope picture taken."

"That's great," said Gloria. "You've got a good day for it."

"Yeah," I said. "I can't wait."

"And now," she said, getting up and brushing sand off the seat of her pants, "I'm heading back. Your grandfather said something about blueberry pancakes. Want to join us?"

When I got home after breakfast, Dad was on the porch reading the paper. "You should've come over," I said, sitting on the rail. "Granddad made pancakes."

"You're right, I should've," said Dad. "It's pretty poor pickings around here."

"Where's Mom?"

"Still asleep."

"Still asleep? How can she be?" I said. "We're supposed to go into Ocean City today. She promised."

"I wouldn't count on it, Hannah. Your mother had a headache last night and I'm not sure she'll be feeling up to it. Anyway, she'll be awake after a while. Now, why don't you go get started on your packing; then you won't have to fool with it later."

I went inside, headed for the closet in the hall, and dragged out my old blue suitcase, bumping and thumping it against the wall. I put my ear up to Mom's door, but I didn't hear anything, and had just started in on my clatter-bang-boom again when Dad called from the porch, "Hannah, what are you doing? You'll wake your mother."

"Yeah," I whispered as I set the suitcase on the floor and pushed open the door to Mom's room. I moved up closer, looking down at the person lying there. Her face was slack and sort of pale, her mouth hanging open and her breath sounding rough, like it was almost a snore.

I watched her for a while, staring hard and willing her to wake up, but when she didn't I tiptoed backwards out of the room.

If I pack everything except what I need for today and tomorrow, and fold it, too, and not just shove it in the bag any which way, and keep the dirty from the clean and maybe even do a load of wash so it'll *all* be clean —then maybe Mom'll wake up soon and remember about going to the beach, just the two of us, and it'll be an okay next-to-last day after all, I bargained, the way I'd started to do lately when I wanted something to happen about Mom. Then I went around my room like a whirlwind, picking up dirty towels and shirts and shorts, dragging my red flowered skirt out from under the bed, and plucking socks off the windowsill. I bunched everything together and took it out to the washer, dropping it in and adding detergent, turning on the water.

Back in my room, I started in on the clean stuff, folding jeans and sweaters and underwear, putting them in the suitcase. I went through the bureau drawers and added my box of earrings, a ton of pennies, buttons, pens, and a strip of funky black-and-white pictures Mandy, Sue, Jessie Lee, and I took in a machine up on the boardwalk one night. Then I packed my books and tapes and my new Walkman in a tote bag that said DOGGY BAG along the side.

When I was done I went out into the hall, listening again at Mom's door, straining my ears to see if she was up and moving around.

Nothing.

Okay, I told myself. Maybe now if I straighten the

whole rest of the place and pick up the papers and unload the dishwasher and load the stuff that's in the sink and take out the trash and polish the sliding glass door so it's clean enough to walk through if you're not being careful—*then* maybe Mom'll wake up and remember about going to the beach.

And I did all that. I puffed the sofa cushions and put the newspapers in the recycling bin. I unloaded the dishwasher, which is a pain, and loaded it again with assorted glasses, Dad's breakfast dishes, and his peanut butter knife. That's because every night, no matter what, my father has a big blob of peanut butter on a knife before he goes to bed. And every night Mom says, "Watch your cholesterol, Charles." Except for the nights when she goes to bed early. Because of a headache, or something.

I grabbed the Windex and a roll of paper towels and went over to the sliding glass door just as Dad was coming in from the porch. "Here," he said, reaching for the towels. "Give me some of those. I'll do the outside —and I'll race you." We each tore off about a thousand squares. We sprayed the door, inside and out; then we started to work. We rubbed and polished and shined. We swooped from one side to the other, making faces through the glass and laughing. We were almost done when my mother came into the room.

"What's all the noise?" she said, holding on to the counter that separated the living room from the kitchen, leaning her head against the wall.

I swung around to face her, speaking into the sudden quiet that seemed to fill the room. "We cleaned the glass door—Dad and I. And before that I emptied the dishwasher and loaded it with dirty stuff and sort of fixed up the living room." I stopped for a minute, waiting for Mom to say something, and when she didn't I started again. Dad came in from the porch and put his hand on my shoulder, but I went on anyway. "And before *that*—after breakfast—I packed up my whole room and folded everything, even my underwear, and I put a load of wash in, and now—"

I stopped. I waited for Mom to say how now we would go to the beach and get lunch from the Alaska stand and have our pictures taken like the tourists did. Because that's the bargain, I wanted to shout. Because that's the bargain I made with myself.

Mom moved across the room and sat down carefully on the couch. She rubbed at a spot on her forehead, over her eyes, and said, "That's nice." Like maybe I'd said that the sun was shining, or that today was Friday.

"Can I get you some coffee, Katherine?" said Dad.

"Tea, maybe, please," she said, and I sat across from her and watched as Dad made the tea and brought it over to her. I sat and watched the whole time while my mother blew on the tea and waited for it to cool and then drank it, sip by sip. I watched as she stopped, looking down into the mug and, finally, putting it on the table. "You know there was something, last night, maybe the cake, that didn't agree with me. I've heard that some people just can't eat chocolate—that it gives them a headache."

"Could be," said Dad, and when I turned to look at him, his head was bent over the crossword puzzle.

"I don't know. Maybe if I eat something now," said Mom. She got up and went to the kitchen area, pouring herself a glass of juice and putting a piece of bread into the toaster oven. When the toast was done she carried it over to the couch, breaking off little pieces and putting them in her mouth one at a time. The room was so quiet I could hear her chewing.

"So, Hannah," said Mom when she had finished. "What are you and the girls doing today?"

"Me?" I said, my voice sounding small and sort of unused. "And the girls?"

"Yes—Mandy and Sue and Jessie Lee. You must have something planned."

I leaned forward and looked at her, like maybe she was teasing me and any minute she would jump up and say, "Joke—joke! Now get your things and let's get out of here."

"Well?" she prodded me.

Remember, I wanted to yell at her, but because it was sometimes hard to know how Mom was going to react to things now, I didn't. I couldn't. *Remember* and say it, how this was going to be our special day, just for the two of us, the way you said it'd be. The way you promised. *Remember. Remember.*

"Oh, well," said Mom, getting up and still moving carefully. "You'll think of something."

"Yeah," I said. "I'll think of something."

I went in my room, closed the door, and sat on the edge of my bed for I don't know how long, staring at the picture of a sailboat on the wall without really seeing it. After a while I got up and peeled off my clothes and put on my bathing suit and brushed my hair. I grabbed my towel and my flip-flops and headed out through the house. Dad was sitting on the porch, working on his lesson plans. "Going to the pool?" he asked.

"Yeah," I said. "I might as well."

"Good idea. Maybe I'll see you up there later on."

Mandy, Sue, and Jessie Lee were sitting along the edge at the deep end when I got to the pool. "Hey, Hannah," called Jessie Lee. "What're you doing here? I thought you were going into Ocean City with your mom today."

"Oh, I changed my mind. That was no big deal." I tossed my stuff onto a chaise and dove into the water, coming up halfway across the pool and calling back to them, "Anyway—how could I miss hanging out with you guys today, huh?"

Three

Mom and Dad and I had breakfast on the porch our last morning at the beach. We sat at the round wooden table with the yellow place mats and the blue-and-white dishes and ate toast.

"Toast?" I said, looking at my plate. "Where's the cereal? The bagels? Or even raisin bread, with icing on the side? Where're the scrambled eggs or frozen waffles?"

"Gone, I'm afraid," said Mom, making a face. "It didn't exactly come out even this year, did it?"

"It never *does*," said Dad and I together. "Any margarine?" he asked.

"No," said Mom. "That's gone, too, but there's plenty of juice, and some jelly here, way down in the bottom of the jar." She held it out to us, laughing in that wind-chimy way she has, and soon Dad and I joined in, and then we were all rocking back and forth and holding on to the edges of the table.

I guess you had to be there. I mean, it probably wasn't really all that funny, except in a way it was because every year Mom has this thing about the end of vacation matching up with the end of the food in the refrigerator and the cupboard—so we won't have to lug stuff home.

"But we could, you know, take things home. Like half a box of cereal or an extra banana," I said, sputtering through my toast crumbs.

"You're right," said Mom. "And I promise you that next year it'll be different. That next year we'll have a bang-up breakfast on the last day, with kippered herrings and omelets and homemade biscuits."

"You say that *every* year," Dad and I chanted together, and then we all started to laugh again and I thought for a minute how good it was when Mom was like this. When her hands didn't shake and she didn't have a headache or anything. How it was almost like we really had stepped out of one of Granddad's Hannah columns.

Mom got up and cleared the table, carrying the dishes inside and calling back, "We're going to take our coffee over and have it with Aunt Pauli and Uncle Bill."

"Yes," said Dad. He stopped for a minute and rooted through the newspaper until he found the crossword puzzle, folding it and slipping it under his arm. "Why don't you go on in and strip the sheets off your bed, Hannah," he said. "And put them in the leaf bag with the rest of the dirty linens. Then set all your things here on the porch so they'll be ready when I go to load the car."

"And come over and say goodbye to everybody when you're done," said Mom as she came outside carrying two fresh cups of coffee. She handed one to Dad and together they started up the path.

After my parents left I went inside and dried the dishes Mom had washed. I put them away and stood for a minute looking around the kitchen and the living room, thinking how they seemed really bare, like we'd already left. Our Monopoly and Scrabble and Pictionary games were packed and waiting on the porch. Dad's books were gone from the coffee table and Mom's cameras from the bookcase. I knew that as soon as we left, the cleaners would come in, and that by tonight another family would be living in the house. It was funny in a way—to think of somebody else sleeping in *my* bed, listening to the same night sounds *I* listened to, and waking in the morning and staring up at my favorite zigzag crack in the ceiling.

After a while I went into my room. I took off the sheets and shoved them down into the bag Dad had left there. I pulled up the spread and smoothed it out, then packed the rest of my clothes. I dragged my stuff out onto the porch and sat for a minute, making a list in my head: shoes, shorts, shirts, bathing suits, slicker, windbreaker. "Windbreaker," I said out loud. And I knew, sure as anything, that I hadn't packed my windbreaker yesterday, that I hadn't even seen my windbreaker since maybe way in the beginning of the month when Mandy and Sue and Jessie Lee and I had stood out on the pier in a northeaster and let the rain slash down around us.

Back in my room, I looked under the bed and in the closet. I moved out into the hall, opening that closet and feeling along the shelf, shifting the ironing board and the vacuum cleaner. After that I checked the rack next to the washer and dryer, then dropped down to my hands and knees, peering into the crawl space behind them. I found my yellow flips-flops I didn't know I'd lost, a pair of mirror sunglasses, and a broken Frisbee. And I found my windbreaker. I'd just gathered everything up and was working my way out of the space when I spotted something far up front and off to the side, sort of buried there in the shadows.

I inched my way forward again, not sure whether to reach for the thing or leave it be. When I got closer I saw that it was a paper shopping bag and I put out my hand, touching it carefully, ready to scream and jump if anything live and horrible popped out at me. The bag rattled and clattered as I dragged it into the light, and when I looked I saw that it was filled with bottles. About a million bottles, all empty, and more than I'd ever seen in my life except in a store or a movie or something. I picked them out one at a time, lining them up and staring at them. *Vodka Vodka Vodka* The labels seemed to dance at me and I sat down hard, trying to figure it out.

It didn't make sense. I mean, Dad and Mom kept vodka in the cupboard, and sometimes other stuff, too. And beer in the refrigerator. But when the bottles were empty they put them in the trash. But these . . . these . . .

Suddenly it was as if I couldn't breathe and I knew, the same as if I'd seen her hide them, that these bottles belonged to my mother. She'd bought them and drunk what was inside, and hidden them away from me and Dad and everybody else. And what I hadn't wanted to believe was staring me in the face.

Vodka Vodka Vodka The labels danced at me again, twisting and turning, so I pulled back, crouching against the dryer. I grabbed at the bottles and started pushing them down into the bag, wishing that I could break them and smash them into pieces and grind the pieces into air.

I got up and out of there as fast as I could, mostly because I wanted to get away from all those bottles— dead soldiers, I'd heard Dad say once, after a party, when he was throwing empties in the trash. I made it onto the porch and stood leaning on the rail, still trying to catch my breath. And I knew, more than anything, that I couldn't have anybody else find what I had found. Not the cleaners or the owners of the cottage, or even Dad on a last-minute inspection to see if we'd forgotten anything.

I went in and got a brown plastic trash bag and dropped the collection of bottles down deep inside. I slung the bag over my shoulder and started for the door when an idea caught at me and made me stop. "What if there are more?" I said out loud into the empty house. "What if they're *everywhere*?" And, moving like I was going someplace I didn't want to go, I went into the living room, looking behind the couch and under the television and in back of the collection of ragged paperbacks on the bookshelf.

Nothing. And I let my breath out all in a whoosh.

I moved on into Mom and Dad's room, pulling out the dresser and hearing a kind of thud. I grabbed at a bottle and shoved it into my bag, and found another under the extra pillows in the spare-room closet. In between I pushed and pulled at things: at beds and chairs and chests of drawers. And then, when I was done, I had to push and pull the other way, putting stuff back and making sure that nobody coming in would know I'd been looking for anything.

Next I took the bag, holding it tight, and went out the door and around the house and into the woods. The trouble was I couldn't go very *far* without running into another house, but I found a spot between a fallen tree and a berry bush and wedged the bag into it. I dug around on the ground, picking up handfuls of leaves and sticks and pine needles and showering them down on it. I dragged out branches and laid them overtop and kicked dirt every which way. Wiping my hands on the seat of my pants, I started back, trying not to look at what I was leaving behind, trying not to think how those bottles'd never biodegrade and how they'd last for years and maybe even unbalance the ecology and it'd be all my fault. Because of Mom.

I went along, slapping at tree trunks and feeling sort of like Mom had handed me this big old ugly secret that I couldn't get rid of, that I didn't know what to do with. And I wished, more than anything, that I could hide it there in the woods, same as I had the empty bottles.

"Here she is," called Dad when I came around to the

front of the house where he was loading the car and Granddad and Gloria and everybody else were standing around watching him. We stayed there for a while saying how this had been the best summer ever and how it'd really flown by, stuff like that—same as we say every year.

Mandy and Sue and Jessie Lee came down the road singing "So long, it's been good to know yuh," locking their arms and making a circle around me, which is something we do every year to whoever is leaving the earliest.

"See you next year," said Jessie Lee, her eyes spilling over with tears.

"If I write you first, you better answer," said Sue.

"Yeah," said Mandy, biting down hard on her lip and looking up at the trees.

And all of a sudden I felt a humongous lump in my throat.

Then everybody was hugging everybody else and we were in the car and heading down the road. I twisted around in the backseat, looking out the window at Gloria and Granddad, at Aunt Pauli and Casey and Uncle Bill, at Mandy and Sue and Jessie Lee. I watched and waved till long after we had turned the corner and I couldn't see them anymore.

We drove for ages without talking, and after a while Dad turned on the radio, to a country-Western station, and sang along, thumping the palm of his hand on the steering wheel in time to the music.

"I hope we didn't forget anything," said Mom.

"No," said Dad, "I double-checked."

And for a minute I wanted to pound on the back of

the front seat and remind her of what we'd forgotten and how I'd hidden it for her out behind the house, under a heap of dirt and sticks and pine needles. Instead I slid down low and closed my eyes and listened to my father sing "This heart is made for achin', this heart is made for breakin'."

Four

Sam was waiting on the front porch when we got home, and after about a minute while we were strangers with each other, we were back to being best friends again.

"Did you have fun?" she asked. "Were those same girls there who're there every year and did you moon-bathe and hang out at the pool and have your birthday party and were there any cute boys around?"

"Yes, yes, yes, yes, yes—and no," I said. "The only boys I saw were as old as my cousin Casey or these really gross nerds who were forever doing cannonballs off the side of the pool."

"Hey, hold on a minute," said Dad. "Gross nerds have a way of growing up. Just wait till next year. I was a gross nerd once, and a master of the cannonball—and look at me now." He posed like some macho type, flexing his muscles, then turned to open the trunk.

"And speaking of next year, Sam," Dad went on, dumping suitcases and plastic bags out onto the lawn, "why don't you come with us sometime. You'd love Ocean Pines, and there's plenty of room."

"Yeah, Mr. Brant," said Sam. "I mean, I'd like that, and my mom'd let me and all—for a little while, anyway."

"Well, it's settled, then," said Mom as she pulled her camera bag out of the car. "Next year, then. Right?"

There was a sort of silence before I said, "Yeah, next year." My voice sounded thin and seemed to waver on the air, so I quick took a deep breath and said, "Right. That'll be awesome." I swung around and picked up the bag of sheets and towels, waited for Dad to unlock the door, and pushed past him, slitting my eyes and giving him a dirty look. I carried the bag down to the cellar and stood for a minute, leaning on the washing machine and breathing in the cool musty air and hoping that by the time I got upstairs Sam would've forgotten about it.

The thing is that I *know* Sam wants to come to the beach with us same as I *want* her to come. Or used to want her to come. It's something we've talked about since we were little and our parents were always saying, "When you're old enough." Only by the time we *were* old enough, Mom had started to change—to drink—to act like she'd never acted before. She's the reason I never want Sam to come with us on vacation, or spend the night here in town anymore, either. Because of what she might say, what she might do. And I couldn't stand it if Sam found out about her. I couldn't stand it even though she is my best friend and we tell each other everything. Almost. That's why I keep making up fake excuses about how Mom and Dad don't like company and the house at Ocean Pines is too small and there isn't room and that it's really a family vacation and she'd be bored out of her tree.

The thing is that Sam thinks my life is wonderfully smooth and uncluttered and not at all like hers, with her three older sisters and two pesty younger brothers. Only with me it's just the opposite—I *love* to go to Sam's, with the noise and the laughter and the way everybody talks at once. And when I'm with Sam and her family I sometimes forget to worry about my mother.

But next summer was ages away. I sighed and shoved it into a corner of my mind and went upstairs. Mom was standing at the kitchen sink stirring a pitcher of orange juice she'd just made and I watched as she poured herself a glass and reached into the cupboard, taking down a bottle and adding a splash of something else.

"What's that?" I said.

She quick put the bottle away and closed the cupboard, turning toward me and holding up her glass. "Orange juice," she said. "Do you want some? You and Sam?"

"What else?" I said, looking at the cupboard and wondering if I'd really seen what I knew I'd seen.

"Orange juice, I told you. What is this—the third

degree?'' said Mom, her voice flaring. She threw open the refrigerator and stood looking in at the empty shelves. "And now I have to go to the store. There's nothing in this house—nothing.''

Just then Sam came into the kitchen. "Come on, Hannah,'' she said. "I'll help you unpack, and when you're done we can go over to my house on account of I have your birthday present waiting for you.''

We dragged my stuff upstairs, where unpacking mostly consisted of dumping everything in the middle of the bedroom floor. What we did do, though, was check my dollhouse. It's really beautiful and all made of wood and looks just like our real house, with the same red door and the same wrap-around porch, the same white curtains and the same flowers in the flower boxes. Dad and Granddad and Mom and Gloria made it for me, way back when I was four, and I know I'm too old for it now except, as Gloria says, "some things you *never* outgrow.'' Anyway, I blew the dust off one room after another and Sam wiped at the roof and the porch and the window ledges of the house with her shirttail. That's the thing: Sam cares about the dollhouse almost as much as I do.

Afterward we went over to her house and she gave me my present—a barrette that was made of something that looked like silver but was more like hammered metal. We went out behind the garage, hiding from her brothers, and talked for ages. She told me how one night this summer Tommy Greene, who's this boy from down the street, came over and rode her to the frozen-yogurt store on the back of his bike (she bought her own yogurt, though). And I told her how one of the nerds doing cannonballs off the side of the pool wasn't such a nerd after all and how I'd written his name seven times in my diary.

The days between the end of vacation and the beginning of school seemed to go really fast. Sam and I just hung out and once I went to the mall with my mother. I got a great-looking purple sweater there, but that's all. Mostly, I guess, because the whole time we were shopping I kept looking at all the other kids and what they were buying and Mom got mad and said why didn't I have a mind of my own and I could just start school with what I already had and we'd come back later and get what I needed. If she had time.

That's another thing. Mom was glad to get back to work and she was busy developing the pictures she'd taken on vacation and setting up her schedule and answering calls from people who wanted her to do jobs for them. Mom's specialties are what she calls art photographs, pictures of weird kinds of shadows and doors and windows and sometimes even clothes hanging on a line. But then she also does weddings and bar mitzvahs and even children's parties. Because of the money.

School started the day after Labor Day, which was not as exciting as it could have been because seventh grade is the middle of middle school and nobody cares that much about us one way or another. But in a way that's good because we're not young enough to be new, or old enough so that the teachers are forever saying, "Set a good example, now—the rest of the school's looking up to you."

My classes are okay, as classes go, and some are even

better than that. Take language arts, for example. For language arts we have Ms. Garcia, who wears these terrific clothes, all sort of layered, and talks in a misty-sounding voice. What I *really* like about her, though, is that she makes us do a ton of writing and then she reads what we've written right away and always picks out just the word or sentence or something that makes it different from everybody else's.

And then there's health. For health we have Miss Duncan, who's a new-to-teaching teacher—I could tell because of the way her nose got red and twitched when she talked, especially the first day. She's already told us that we're going to discuss sex and AIDS and condoms, and I know, besides that, there'll be something about "personal hygiene"—taking showers and using deodorant. Stuff like that.

Another thing that Miss Duncan said we were going to "put heavy emphasis on" was drug awareness, and alcohol awareness, too. And when she said that about alcohol awareness I thought of the bottles I'd left in the woods at Ocean Pines and felt my face getting red and wondered if everyone could see it.

Five

It was the first part of October before I knew it. That's when Mom invited me to go to the wedding. Well, she didn't actually invite me, it's just that she was going as the photographer and she said I could come along and carry her stuff and sort of help. I think it was mostly because Dad had an all-day teachers' seminar and sometimes Mom gets weird and overly protective and doesn't want me hanging out too long by myself.

Mom woke me early on Saturday, and that's when I found out that if you go to a wedding as a photographer you don't just go to a wedding. I mean, first we had to go to the bride's house, and when we got there everybody was running around in bathrobes and sweatsuits and stuff and saying how they'd never be ready, not in a million years.

Mom said that's the way things were with weddings and by the time twelve o'clock came everybody'd be dressed and beautiful and we'd all be at the church waiting for the music to start. Meanwhile she wandered around the first floor of the house, looking to see which rooms had the best light and trying to decide where to set up her pictures.

The bridesmaids started drifting down the stairs, carrying shoes and hairbrushes and still fastening each other up the back. The parents came next, and finally, after ages, the bride started down the steps. She was so beautiful, all in clouds of white with some kind of crown thing on her head, that for a minute there was this awesome silence while the father went forward and held out his hand to his daughter and it was all so incredibly sad and happy both at the same time.

After that everybody started talking at once, with the bridesmaids jabbering like monkeys in the zoo and the bride saying did she look all right and the father telling jokes that weren't very funny, and the mother handing out the flowers and saying weren't they lovely and did anyone think it was going to rain and should she take umbrellas.

That's when Mom did something magical. I don't know how she did it and I didn't see her do anything special, but all of a sudden she had everyone in the living room. I mean, the bridesmaids had their shoes on and the bride stopped looking in the mirror and the mother sat down and sighed and said how it was sure to be a perfect wedding after all and the father told a joke that made everybody laugh. Then Mom started in on the pictures: of the bride with the bridesmaids and with her sister and her little brother and pinning a boutonniere on her father's lapel and a corsage on her mother's purse, and one even by herself standing in front of a window and looking dreamy. And when the limousine came we all went outside and Mom opened the door on one side and took a picture of the bride getting in from the other side.

After that, Mom and I got in our car and raced for the church so we'd be there in time to get a picture of the bride getting *out* of the limo. Once we got to the church Mom told me just to go in and find a seat somewhere in back, that she had to take pictures during the service and be almost invisible while she was doing it, and that she'd see me later.

When the ceremony was over we made another mad dash—this time for some fancy club downtown where the reception was being held. And going inside there was like stepping into a movie. A band was playing and waiters and waitresses were walking around with trays of food that Mom said were hors d'oeuvres and just the beginning, and bars were set up all over the place.

"Good," said Mom, heading for the one closest to the door. "I need a drink—after this morning. Come on, Hannah-banana, and you can have a Coke." She asked the bartender for a vodka and tonic and drank it down, almost like it was water. "Now, let's go try and round up everybody for some more pictures," she said, putting her glass on the corner of the bar and heading out into the hall.

The hall was large, with a gigantic fireplace and this wonderful staircase that kind of swooped down from high overhead. And Mom worked her magic again. She was everywhere, bending, stretching, stooping, kneeling, and taking pictures of the wedding party in various combinations.

When she was partway done, the father of the bride came up and said, "I bet I know a hardworking photographer who could use a drink. Right?"

For a minute I thought sure Mom would say how she'd already had one, that she had work to do. But instead she put her hand up to her throat and laughed and said in a scratchy voice, "A little vodka'd be just great. And tonic, please." And then she was off, running up the steps for about the fiftieth time, fluffing the bride's dress and showing her how to hold her flowers. By the time she came down, the bride's father was back, carrying a Coke for me, my mother's drink, and a plate of shrimp.

Mom handed me the shrimp, held her glass in both hands, took a big swallow, and said, "Wonderful. Simply wonderful."

"Well, good," said the man. "That's the way it's supposed to be—and there's plenty more where that came from."

After the pictures in the hall were finished we went into the main room and just sort of wandered around. It was weird in a way: I mean, being at a party and not knowing anybody there. "What do we do now?" I asked.

"Oh, just hang out for a while, till after the meal, and take some pictures of interesting-looking people and hope they're the people the bride's family want pictures *of*. Some families even give me a list: Aunt Tillie, Uncle Albert, the cousins from Pittsburgh.''

I laughed, looking into the crowd and thinking of my mother worming her way through it and trying to find somebody's Aunt Tillie or Uncle Albert, or even the cousins from Pittsburgh. When I turned she was gone, and I stood there for a moment, feeling the way I had once when I was little and I lost her at the circus. Then I saw her coming toward me, calling my name and waving her glass. And the glass was full.

Next thing I knew, a waitress was going through the crowd hitting on a gong and saying that the buffet was open. I was starving, but Mom said we had to wait and let the guests go first. Eventually we got at the end of the line, which just inched along and was sort of boring —but not for my mother. I mean she started talking to this man and woman in front of us and soon they were laughing and joking like maybe they'd known each other for a thousand years. Once Mom rocked back on her heels and the man caught her and spun her around and said what they all needed was another drink and maybe he'd better go and see to that. He did, and when he came back he said something to Mom and she laughed a spirally kind of laugh that floated out over the whole entire room and sounded louder than everybody else put together. My face burned and I stared at the floor and tried not to see if anybody was looking at us.

We got our food and I followed Mom and her new friends to a table at the far side of the room. Mom carried her plate out like a tray, with her glass sitting in the middle of it. But there was plenty of room because the only things she'd taken to eat were olives and celery and a couple of carrot sticks.

The music started up again after we ate and Mom had to hurry off to take a picture of the bride and groom's first dance. I stayed where I was at the table, but in a while I began to feel extra, so I went into the other room and found a place next to the dance floor, but hidden under a giant potted palm. It was fun being there, and I watched the dancing and listened to the music and felt the beat coming up through the floor-boards. From time to time, Mom would dart out and take a picture. Once, when she passed close to where I was standing, I saw that she had taken her shoes off and that she had a sheen of sweat on her face.

When they started playing a bunch of slow songs I decided that that was as good a time as any to go and find the bathroom. It was down the stairs and had this really pretty parlor in front. I was just finishing up when I heard two women come in.

"Well, my dear," said one, in a voice that sounded like what I think a cat would sound like if a cat could talk, "I'd hate to see *those* pictures."

"What pictures?" said the other.

"The wedding pictures."

"Why's that?"

"Haven't you noticed?" said the cat woman. "The photographer's positively sloshed. I mean pickled. Blotto."

And I stood in my stall, holding on to the walls and trying to keep the world from going around and waiting for them to leave so they'd never, in a million years, know that I was there.

When I got back to the reception, all of a sudden it wasn't fun anymore and I wanted it to be over. I wanted to take my mother and get out of there, except that was a lie because what I *really* wanted was to get out of there by myself. And maybe just to keep on going.

Instead I found my place under the potted palm again, pushing far into the shadows. The music was loud. It banged and crashed around me and made my teeth hurt. My shoes pinched my feet and my legs ached from standing. After a while I crept out into the light and went to sit at an empty table, looking around at all the women in the room, trying to tell which one was the cat woman.

The music stopped and the blur of color on the dance floor turned into people and the people fanned themselves and wiped their brows and moved to the edges of the room. I saw my mother throw her arm over some man's shoulder and lean up against him. She caught sight of me and called out, "Having fun, Hannah-banana? Some party, huh?"

One of the musicians played an attention-getting thing on a horn and said, "And now, ladies and gentlemen—the bride will cut the cake." The crowd clapped and moved forward.

I saw my mother struggling with her camera, dropping the strap of the case over her shoulder and listing to one side. As if it was all really heavy, which I knew it wasn't. Then she was fighting her way through the people, yelling, "Beep beep, here I come!" When she got to the front, the bride was just feeding a piece of cake to the groom while he fed one to her at the same time. My mother yelped and tried to focus her camera, lunging forward, slipping and going down, catching hold of the table where the cake was. For a minute there was a terrible thick silence while the cake and the toy bride and groom on top swayed back and forth. Then everybody gasped and moved at once.

A waitress caught the cake, smushing her hand into the icing on the side, while several others steadied the table. A man reached down to help my mother up off the floor and a bridesmaid chased a lens under a chair. From deep in the crowd, somebody laughed. Hah hah hah hah hah. And the sound seemed to be caught up and echoed through the room.

The bride and groom went off and changed into real clothes, and when they came back the bride danced with her father and she cried and he cried. My mother stood carefully, as if balanced on a trampoline, and took a picture. Then the bride reached for her new husband's hand and they ran out the front door with everybody following along behind and throwing birdseed.

After that the wedding reception was over. I mean, people milled around for a few minutes but the musicians were already packing their instruments and the waiters were gathering up about a ton of glasses.

I was standing there just watching everything and wondering where Mom was when the mother of the bride came up to me. "Aren't you the photographer's daughter?" she asked, holding Mom's shoes out to me.

And for a minute I wanted to scream, "No!" For a minute I wanted to say that I'd never seen her before today, that I didn't even know her name. Then I felt bad for thinking that and swallowed hard and said, "Yes, I'm her—she's my mother."

"Well, you tell your mother that those pictures had better be good. Now, don't you think it's time for the two of you to get on home." When she talked, it sounded as if her nose was sort of pinched, like maybe she smelled something rotten.

"Get on home." The words stuck in my head. "Get on home. Get on home." I looked across the room and saw Mom sitting on a chair against the wall, her head back, a glass in her hand. I started over to her and then it was as though something had hold of my legs and I couldn't go any farther. "Get on home," I thought again. But how?

And I knew more than anything that I didn't want to ride in the car with my mother. Knew more than anything that my mother shouldn't *drive* a car.

Six

Maybe the car won't start, I told myself. I mean, cars sometimes don't, except that's mostly when it's cold outside, or the battery's dead. I couldn't call my father because he wasn't home—and anyway, what would I say? I thought about Gloria and how maybe I could explain the whole thing to her and ask her to come get us and take us home. But I didn't want her to see Mom this way. There was always the bride's family or one of the musicians. And for a minute I could almost hear myself telling them how we'd lost the keys, asking if they would just drop us off. I knew I wouldn't, though.

I was still standing there, feeling trapped, like maybe

a giant cage had slammed down around me, and didn't see Mom till she was standing beside me. "Come on, Hannah," she said. "This party's over. Let's get out of here."

Mom had struggled into her shoes and we were all the way out on the sidewalk before I got up enough nerve to say to my mother that maybe we ought to take a taxi home.

"A taxi? Are you crazy?" she said, her voice sounding high and shrill, so that people going by on the street turned to look at her. "We have a car. It's right here—somewhere."

She dropped her camera bag onto the ground, swinging around, lurching and reaching to catch hold of a street sign. "I parked it under a sign, like this one," she said, shaking the post. "What the hell've they done with it?"

"Maybe it was towed away," I said, crossing my fingers and wishing for it to be true. "Maybe the sign said 'No Parking' and it was towed away."

"No," said Mom. She headed up the street and then came back, catching me by the arm and leaning close, her face up against mine. "You know, don't you?" she said. "You know and you won't tell me. I told you it was your job. That's all you had to do—keep track of the car—and now you won't tell me." Her voice cracked and I closed my eyes.

The cage tightened around me. I mean, I *knew* where the car was, but maybe if I said I didn't we could just keep looking for a while and then take a taxi home after all. Mom pushed at me and I stepped off backwards into the street. She turned and started across the sidewalk.

"I'm going for the manager of this club," she said, pronouncing her words carefully, with lots of space around them. "My car's gone and I *want* the manager."

"No, Mom, wait," I said, running to catch up with her. "I know where it is. I just remembered." I took her by the arm and picked her stuff up off the sidewalk, and together we went around the corner and down the hill to the car.

Mom drove slowly, inching along, so that people blew horns at her and shook their fists and yelled out rolled-down windows that maybe she should get a horse. Except that when we got to traffic lights she speeded up, sliding through sometimes after they had turned red, so that all around us there was a screeching of brakes. She drove in a wavery line, swinging over close to cars parked along the curb till I was sure we were going to crash, then veering out suddenly into the oncoming lane.

I dug my fingernails into the palms of my hand and held my breath and prayed my seat belt would work and wished for an air bag. I jammed my feet hard against the floorboards and thought how maybe I could open the door and jump out. But I knew I couldn't. Maybe a policeman'll see us, I told myself. See us and make us stop and then he'll give us a ride home in his car and everything will be all right. Only I knew it wouldn't because I'd once seen a show on TV where a cop stopped a driver for weaving all over the road and made him walk a straight line and breathe into a Breathalyzer that told whether he'd been drinking or not. And I didn't want that to happen to Mom. No matter what.

We turned off University Parkway and all of a sudden

it was as if she thought she was on some kind of a speedway.

"Mom—wait—don't you think—" I cried out.

"Think, think, think, you think too much, Hannah Jane," my mother said. "What you should do is just go with the flow. That's it—just go with the flow." She pushed a button and the windows shot the rest of the way down and air poured into the car. She pressed even harder on the accelerator. I closed my eyes and kept them squeezed tight as we sailed around corners and bounced along streets in the neighborhood. I kept them closed till we were at the end of our driveway and had banged into the garage door, denting it.

"There," said Mom as she got out of the car and headed for the house. I grabbed the camera bag and followed her.

When we got inside I had to go to the bathroom, and while I was upstairs I changed my clothes, taking off my good dress and shoes, pulling on jeans and a sweater and sneakers. The red light was blinking on the answering machine in the hall, and I rewound the tape and stood listening to my father tell how his meeting was running late and that he'd be home after a while; to Sam saying that she was bored out of her mind and to call her the absolute first minute I walked in the door. I didn't.

When I got downstairs again, Mom had made herself a drink and carried it into the living room. She was sitting on the couch, and she was crying. And the weird thing was that I didn't know what to do, or where to look. I guess that's mostly because I didn't ever remember seeing Mom cry before, except at movies and stuff like that.

"I should be taking pictures for *National Geographic*," she said, sniveling and wiping her nose on the back of her hand. "I should be going out on assignments, to exotic places, and taking pictures of mountains and waterfalls and erupting volcanoes. And do you know what I'm doing? Do you? Do you?"

I didn't answer her, but Mom went on anyway. "I'm taking pictures of weddings," she said, sort of spitting out the word *weddings*.

"I'm taking pictures of weddings and kiddie birthday parties when I should be having exhibits—in museums —and galleries." Tears rolled down her face and she hiccuped. Then she put her head back and went to sleep.

I sat for a long time and watched my mother sleep and then I got up and tiptoed over, reaching for the glass, trying to ease it out of her hand. Suddenly she twisted away, pulling back on the glass and dumping it onto the sofa. I watched the liquid form a puddle before it sank into the cushion. Then I took the empty glass out of her hand and put it on the table.

What if somebody came to the door, I thought. What if Sam came, or Granddad, or Aunt Pauli or Mrs. Porter from next door? What would I say then? I shook my mother hard and said, "Mom, come on. Let's go upstairs so you can take a nap—so you can sleep in a real bed."

"Sleep," she mumbled, rolling over onto the couch and drawing her feet up. "Sleep."

I grabbed at her, pulling her arm, her shoulder, till she finally sat up, swaying there on the edge of the seat like some big old floppy rag doll. "Come on," I said. "You've got to get up."

She looked at me and blinked and sort of threw herself to her feet, falling into me, so that together we staggered out to the hall and up the stairs. She slid along the wall, knocking against a photograph of a sea gull she had taken and sending it crashing down the steps. When we got to her room she collapsed onto the bed, curling into a ball.

I went downstairs and sat and stared at the couch where my mother had been and thought about Granddad and wondered what he'd write in the Hannah column if he could see me now. Then I got up and turned the sofa cushion wet side under. I picked the rest of the glass out of the picture frame and hung it back on the wall, hoping Dad wouldn't notice. I'd just gone into the kitchen to get the dustpan when Sam called.

"Come on over," she said. "My parents are going out but we can order in a pizza, they said, and then, when the kids are done seeing *Jungle Book*, we can watch a movie."

I stared at the door and knew, more than anything, that I wanted to run right out of it and over to Sam's. Then I thought of my mother upstairs and how maybe I shouldn't leave her like that. "I can't," I said.

"Why?" asked Sam.

Why? I said inside my head. Why? Why? Why? "Because I have to do my homework," I said.

"Your homework?" said Sam. "On Saturday night?"

"Yeah, well, I took this really long book for book reports and I haven't even *started* it."

"Yuck," said Sam.

After we hung up I turned away from the phone, taking the vodka bottle out of the cupboard and emptying it down the sink. Then I filled the bottle with water and put it back.

I was sitting in the sun porch watching a show about penguins when my father came home.

"Where's your mother?" he said.

"Upstairs. She's asleep," I said.

"Doesn't she feel well? Is she all right?"

"Yeah," I said. "I mean, well, she had a . . . headache."

Dad went to sit on the rocking chair, sighing and putting his head back, rubbing his forehead.

And for a minute I wanted to be little again and able to run and sit on his lap. I wanted to tell him about the wedding and the cat woman in the bathroom and what she said and about Mom nearly knocking the cake over and how she hung on to people and talked louder than she should've. I wanted to tell him about the ride home. I didn't, though, because Dad had never said anything to me about what was happening to Mom and maybe I wasn't *supposed* to know. Or maybe I was the only one who *did* know. Me and the cat woman.

Seven

I thought about the cat woman a couple of weeks later, when I came in from eating supper over at Sam's one night. Mom had the wedding pictures spread out all over the dining room table—and they were good.

"Come look, Hannah," said Dad, who was standing beside her, picking up the pictures one at a time. "These will mean even more to you, because you were there."

At first I hung back, afraid to move closer. Ever since that Saturday I'd shut my mind down tight on the wedding, trying never to think of it. The weird thing was that Dad'd never mentioned the dent in the garage door or the missing glass on the photograph on the stairway. And the even weirder thing was that Mom had never said anything about that day either—even how the vodka bottle was suddenly filled with water.

"Well," said Dad, waiting. And I took a deep breath, moving over to the table, looking down. I blinked, and blinked again, as the pictures I'd been carrying in my head—of my mother on the floor, or leaning against some man she didn't know, or reaching for a glass— gave way to the bride, the groom, the candlelight and flowers.

"They're good, Mom," I said, reaching out with my finger to trace the lettering on the albums sitting on the table. *Our Wedding. Our Daughter's Wedding. Our Son's Wedding.*

"Yes indeed," said Dad. "She's a very talented lady, your mother is." And Mom made a mumbly noise, the way you do when someone pays you a compliment and you don't think you should take it but you know it's true.

"Magic," I said. And for a minute I remembered how it had been at the wedding, with Mom getting everybody together and making the pictures come out right. Before the day got old and the magic wore away. For me, anyway.

Mom sorted the pictures into piles and Dad sat and watched as she put them into the albums. "I'm going to run over and deliver these tonight," she said. "I called to say I was coming, so I hope the bride and groom'll have a chance to be there. It's more fun to look at them all together." She blew a speck of dust off a scene in the church and slid it into place.

"You're missing one," said Dad.

"Missing one?" said Mom. "All these pictures, how can I be missing one?"

"Well, maybe not missing," said Dad. "But don't you usually have a shot of the bride cutting the cake toward the end of the album? You know, the way you have the bridal bouquet in the front and the bride and groom's clasped hands with the wedding rings showing somewhere in the middle."

"It blurred," said Mom. "They were fooling around, stuffing cake into each other's mouths, practically *refusing* to stand still. I don't know how I'm supposed to get a picture of *that*."

"You generally manage, though, don't you?" said Dad. "That's what you're so good at."

"What are you saying, Charles?" said Mom, her voice suddenly hard and thin-edged. "If you don't like my work, just get away. Stop hanging over me."

"I *do* like it—I told you so," said Dad. He picked up the picture of the bride dancing with her father and said, "Wow, they're sure looking dejected in this one."

"Dejected?" said Mom, grabbing the picture out of his hand and slamming it down on the table. "They were crying, for heaven's sake."

"I just said they were dejected—I didn't say you *made* them that way."

"That's what you meant," said Mom. "I can tell. And I suppose you think it's all fun and games, trailing around at other people's weddings. Not knowing anybody. Not having anything to do."

I wanted to kick my father under the table and tell him to keep quiet. But I didn't have the energy and I turned away, heading into the kitchen for a glass of water.

Ever since school that afternoon I'd had a headache and felt hot and cold, both at the same time. And now my throat was starting to hurt. I stood at the sink, taking tiny sips of water and trying to swallow without actually swallowing. From the hall, I heard Mom get her coat out of the closet, heard her call that she was going to deliver the pictures, that she'd be back in a while.

"Much homework tonight?" asked Dad when I wandered into the sun porch, where he was watching "Jeopardy" and calling out the questions quicker even than any of the contestants on the show.

"Well, I did some over at Sam's, before supper, and all that's left is I have to write this thing for creative writing, only I don't feel so good and right now I'm just thinking because almost the biggest part of writing is the thinking. That's what Granddad sometimes says, anyway."

"Just don't do so much thinking you forget to write," said Dad, reaching over and feeling my forehead with the palm of his hand. "I don't know—but you may have a fever. We'll see what your mother thinks when she gets home. And what's the topic, for this thing for creative writing?"

" 'My Deepest Secret That I'm Willing to Share,' " I said.

"I thought the point of a secret was that you didn't have to share," said Dad.

"Yeah, well, Ms. Garcia said that, too. That's why she put 'Willing to Share' in the title. And, I mean, if we don't want to do that, then we can just write about some minor secret, like how M&M's are my favorite comfort food.''

''What's a comfort food?''

''Oh, you know, what you eat to make yourself feel good,'' I said.

''Peanut butter,'' said Dad. ''And are M&M's really yours?''

''I guess,'' I said, but by then he'd turned back to Final Jeopardy and was trying to decide, if he were the champion with $9,200, what he'd wager on Greek mythology.

I sat for a minute, half listening to the TV and half thinking about comfort foods. I knew Sam'd pick butterscotch brownies for hers, and Gloria'd pick lemon drops, and Granddad, maybe, those big hard pretzels.

Mom'd say vodka. The thought popped into my head and sort of drummed there. *Mom'd say vodka.* I knew she probably would even though vodka was vodka, and not a food at all.

And then I thought about ''My Deepest Secret That I'm Willing to Share'' again and about Ms. Garcia and wondered what would happen if for my homework I just sort of spilled it all out to her. About how I think —how I know—my mother sometimes drinks too much and I'm not sure what to do and maybe I'll explode if I don't get to talk to somebody about it soon. How Sam and I aren't as good friends as we used to be because of this and how I'm not sure whether Dad knows or not, and if he doesn't, then I don't want him to. Except he should. Somebody should. I thought about writing it all down and Ms. Garcia taking it home with the other school papers and reading it and how she might not know what to do either and just end up sending me to the guidance counselor. And I knew I couldn't do that. Never in a million years. I mean, somebody might *see* me.

Dad was yelling at the TV set, calling "Way to go" to the guy who'd just won another $9,200. He picked up the remote control, skipping to CNN, and, when a commercial came on, to a bunch of other channels, looking for a movie he hadn't seen yet, and back to the news again. Just then we heard Mom at the front door, but instead of coming in where we were she went on to the kitchen, and in a minute I heard the clatter of ice cubes.

"That was a quick trip," said Dad when she finally came into the sun porch.

"Yes," said Mom.

"Did they like the pictures?"

"I wouldn't know." She drank her drink halfway down and stood for a minute, shaking her head. "When I got there I rang the bell and this person I'd never seen before came to the door—not Mr. Phillips, or Mrs. Phillips either. And then she, the person, handed me a check and took the pictures and said they'd be in touch if they needed more and, wham, shut the door. And me standing there with my mouth open. I mean, not a 'Won't you please come in,' or 'It's good to see you again,' or 'We can't wait to see these pictures.' Nothing. Zip. After the way I worked on their stupid wedding." She finished her drink, holding her head back and draining the glass, as if to get every drop.

"But I don't understand," said Dad. "They were such great pictures, and people always ask you in and half the time they have a whole list of their friends who might want some work done."

"You meet all kinds in this business," said Mom as she headed for the kitchen. I thought for a minute how the mother of the bride had come up to me after the wedding and said what she did, about Mom and me getting on home. And how maybe she had known what the cat woman knew. About my mother, I mean. I got up and sort of slithered out of the room, hoping Dad wouldn't notice and remember to tell her I wasn't feeling well.

Up in my room I took out my notebook and scribbled something about M&M's being my secret comfort food, but just the thought of those hard little candies made my throat hurt, and I gave up and went to bed.

When I woke the next morning my throat was so sore I could hardly swallow, and my pillow felt hot and sweaty under my head. I turned off the clock and then, when it rang a few minutes later, on account of the snooze alarm, I turned it off again. More than anything, I wanted to tell someone how bad I felt, so I crawled out of bed and made my way into my parents' room. Dad was in the shower and I could hear him singing over the sound of the water, the same song he sings every morning that's all in German and about someone named Augustine. I knew that things must've been okay last night because on the days when Mom has a headache he just tiptoes around and tries not to make any noise at all.

Mom was still asleep, and I stood next to her side of the bed and sort of nudged it with my knee. "Mom," I croaked. "I don't feel good and my throat hurts something awful."

She reached for me and pulled me down and felt my head kind of all at the same time. "Oh, Hannah, you're burning up," she said. Next thing I knew, she was out of bed and had tucked me in her place, which is about the only good thing I can say about getting sick—being in Mom and Dad's big bed. In the daytime, anyway. She turned on the TV to one of those morning shows that's mostly commercials and weather reports, but that was okay because it gave me a comfortable feeling. She put on her robe and started for the door, saying that she would call the doctor as soon as the office was open, and that she'd bring me some juice.

"Oh, no, it'll hurt," I said, swallowing carefully and trying not to think of the juice and how it'd feel prickling all the way down. And then I slept some and was awake some and things happened all in a blur. I remember Dad getting dressed for work and stooping to kiss me goodbye and pretending my head was so hot it burned his mouth. I remember Mom coming back with crushed ice in a mug and telling me we had a twelve o'clock appointment with Dr. Kelly. And I remember the morning sort of skidding along with Mom in and out of the room and the sounds of the phone and the TV and a car out on the street all jumbled together.

When it was time to go to the doctor, Mom helped me get dressed and her hands were cool and gentle. I thought of the time last summer at Ocean Pines when we found this injured bird on a path and Mom knelt down beside it and cupped it in her hands and moved it out of the way and over under a bush. I had stood there for ages watching my mother with the bird, and the thing is that that's how I felt, right now. Like the bird, I mean. And I wondered why she couldn't always be this way and why she sometimes forgot things and fell and yelled and when she talked sounded like she had a mouthful of paste. And whether it was my fault and what I should do about it. Except I couldn't think of anything to do.

Then my head hurt more than it had before and I sat on the edge of the bed, but Mom caught my hand and pulled me up and said, "Come on, Hannah-banana. Let's go see Dr. Kelly so he can get you feeling better."

The trouble with Dr. Kelly is that he's a pediatrician and I think by now I should be seeing a grownup doctor, only every time I ask Mom she says how I've been going to him for ages and he knows me really well, and besides that, she went to him when *she* was a little girl. Only I don't see what difference that makes.

When we walked into the waiting room I felt like some kind of a giant with all the baby-size chairs and tables and the million toys and a bunch of kids all slobbering and crying and sucking their thumbs. I went over to the corner, as far as I could get from everyone, and sat staring up at a picture of poison ivy that had been there probably forever. And when it was my turn to go into the office I got up and looked over my shoulder and sort of hissed at my mother that I'd go by myself. I mean, it was bad enough to go to a *baby* doctor without having my mother come *in* with me.

Dr. Kelly was small and seemed to get smaller every time I saw him. He had one of those haircuts like

Marines have, as if someone had taken a shaver to his head, and his ears stuck out on the sides. He was nice and all, though, and I guess it wasn't his fault that I didn't want to come to him anymore.

"Well, Hannah," he said, sitting back and making a steeple with his fingers. "Understand you're not feeling so well today."

"No," I said. "I mean yes, I'm not."

Then he took my temperature and looked in my eyes and ears and finally my throat. He made me say "Ahhhh" and pushed down on my tongue with one of those Popsicle-stick things until I almost gagged. "That's some mean-looking throat you've got there," he said. "It's probably strep, but we'll take a culture and see what grows. Meanwhile we'll start you on some antibiotics." He reached for his stethoscope and said, "Now just let me listen to your chest."

"My chest?" I squeaked, locking my arms across the front of me.

"Yes," he said. "To make sure there's no congestion."

"There's not."

"You're probably right," he said. "But let's just make sure, shall we?"

I thought about saying no and just sitting there forever, but after a while I unlocked my arms and Dr. Kelly peeled up my shirt and moved the stethoscope around me, saying, "Deep breath, now," over and over. And the whole time he was doing that, I was staring somewhere over his left ear and thinking how maybe I'd die of embarrassment and how he was probably thinking that I, Hannah Jane Brant, was the flattest-chested person in the whole entire world.

"Chest sounds fine," he said, turning back to his desk and writing out a prescription. Then he made his finger steeple again and said, "Everything else going along okay, Hannah?"

And for a minute I felt as if somebody had given me this humongous key and it was up to me to turn it. I mean, Dr. Kelly was a doctor and you're supposed to be able to say things to doctors and all I had to do was tell him about my mother and how maybe sometimes she drank too much and then he'd tell me what to do and then I'd do it and after that everything'd be okay. I took a deep breath and pushed the words around inside my head, trying to shape them into sentences. But when they came out they sounded small and wimpy. "It's just that—there is one thing—I mean, with my mother and how—"

"Yes indeed, your mother's a wonderful woman," Dr. Kelly said. "I've known her all her life. She used to come in, to this very office, but then you know that. And I'm always sure I can count on the Brants not to have any major problems. Right?" He got up without waiting for me to answer and went over to the door, opening it and beckoning for my mother to come inside.

"Hello, Katherine," he said. "Good to see you, though I'm afraid Hannah here has a strep throat. But we'll just put her on an antibiotic, and in a few days she'll be good as new." I stood there listening to him telling Mom to keep me home tomorrow and through the weekend and asking about Dad and what she was working on. I stared at him as hard as I could and said, again and again, inside my head, "*Look* at me. *Listen* to me."

He didn't, though, except to say, "Well, Hannah, I guess you're too big for something from the present drawer, aren't you?"

"Yeah," I said as I followed my mother out of the office.

We stopped at the Giant Store on the way home and Mom ran in to get the prescription filled. I waited in the car, wishing the whole time that she'd hurry up and that we'd get home fast and that she'd give me my medicine and that I'd soon be well. I scrunched down in my seat, resting my knees on the dashboard and closing my eyes, thinking how tomorrow, or when I felt better, I'd do my writing assignment over. And this time I'd really, truly write "My Deepest Secret That I'm Willing to Share."

All about how I hate Dr. Kelly.

Eight

The next day I was better, but not really well. My head felt cottony and far away and my throat still hurt, but not as much as it had before and not enough to keep me from eating the milk toast Mom made. One thing I have to say straight out, though: I have mixed feelings about milk toast. I mean, how could you like a piece of toast with a blob of butter sitting on top and the whole thing floating in a bowl of hot milk. It's gross-looking, and sort of slimy going down, but in a disgusting kind of way it tastes good. Or maybe it's just that it makes me *feel* good, and taken care of. Like strong arms wrapped around me.

Anyway, Mom brought the milk toast upstairs on a tray and served it to me in her bed with a bunch of pillows in back of me and the television on, so all of a sudden I felt like Lady Astor, or Princess Di, or someone.

"Enjoy being spoiled," she said, setting the tray on my lap and smiling, "because the next meal you eat will be downstairs, at the kitchen table."

"Yeah," I said, settling back on the pillows and wiggling my toes under the covers.

Then Mom sat on the foot of the bed and got a sort of serious look on her face. "Now, Hannah, I have a bit of a problem today," she said. "I have a job down at the Hyatt, taking pictures for a retirement luncheon, and I hate to leave you here alone. So what do you think— shall I call Gloria and see if she can come over and stay with you? If she's not doing anything, I'm sure she wouldn't mind and—"

"Mo—m," I said. "I'm twelve years old. I'll be fine." Only the whole time I was saying it I was thinking what I'd really truly like would be for Gloria to come over and how, if she did, we could play the word games she always knows and take turns reading to each other, a chapter at a time, from one of my books.

"You sure?" said Mom.

"Positive," I said, crossing my fingers and toes, both at the same time.

"Well, good," she said, getting up and going to the closet, taking out a skirt and a turtleneck. "I've made a sandwich for your lunch and left it in the refrigerator, and you can fix yourself a Coke. And I'll call from downtown."

When she was dressed and ready to go, Mom spent ages reminding me not to answer the door and if anybody called just to tell them that my mother couldn't come to the phone and to take a message and not to say, under any circumstances, that I was in the house alone. And then, once she was done, she told it to me all over again.

After Mom had gone I settled back in bed to watch a talk show about divorced parents who all had joint custody of their kids and how they divided them up (the kids, I mean) sort of like a peanut butter sandwich, with half for the mother and half for the father. It made me sad and I felt sorry for the children and wondered what it'd be like to live in two places instead of one and how they'd ever remember where they were supposed to go, and when.

I picked up my book and tried to read, but the voices of the mothers and fathers on the TV seemed to get louder and louder and push between me and the words on the page. I turned off the set, but then the quiet was louder than the noise had been. Soon I began to hear creakings and settling sounds, as if the house was sighing around me. I got up and started down the stairs, stopping on just about every step and leaning over the banister and listening again and thinking how maybe I didn't really like being home alone in the middle of the morning, when everybody was someplace else. I checked the locks on all the doors and went to stand by the front window, watching Mrs. Miller from across the street walking her roly-poly sausage dog. I sat on the couch and listened to the clock tick and looked at the dust motes hanging there in the sunlight.

After a while I went into the kitchen and ate my lunch and some leftover cold spaghetti I found in the refrigerator. And when I was done it was only eleven-thirty—and I wondered what to do for the rest of the day.

Upstairs again, I stood at the window in my parents' room and watched Mrs. Miller coming back the other way. I studied the pictures stuck around the mirror on my mother's dresser and tried on a bunch of her beads and a big pair of hoop earrings and even some eyeliner, except that I smudged it and ended up wiping it all off. I flopped across the bed and turned on the TV again, but it was mostly soaps and news. Dullsville. I picked up the books on the bedside table and thought how they were fat and boring-looking and how I was never going to read grownup books, even when I was a grownup.

I stared at the phone and wished that it would ring and almost called Gloria. But I didn't. I picked up the yellow pages and flipped through them, which may sound odd except that reading the phone book is what I do sometimes when I don't have anything else to do. Or don't feel like doing what I'm supposed to do. I mean, you can find a lot of stuff in the phone book, like how many Domino's Pizza places there are in Baltimore and where to order balloons, if you want to order balloons, and who sells tombstones. I started at the back and looked through tropical fish and restaurants and flea markets and animal hospitals and was just about to close the book when I saw the word ALCOHOLISM at the top of a page. And the next page, and the one after that.

"Alcoholism." I whispered it, then said it out loud. "Alcoholism." I closed my mouth and the word seemed to spin and change around me.

"Alcoholism. Alcohol. Alcoholic." I thought of my mother and how she made milk toast and brought it to me in bed and how she couldn't be an alcoholic, never in a million years. Then I remembered the empty bottles I'd found hidden around the beach house. I looked down at the book, running my finger along the pages, saying the words under my breath. "Recovery Resources . . . Residential Treatment . . . Outpatient Programs . . ."

I went back to the beginning of the list and started over and that's when I saw it. Just one skinny little part that said: "Alcoholism: 24-hour HELPline," with the HELP in capital letters, as if it was written specially for me. There was even a phone number, with the word "toll-free" in front of it, and I grabbed paper and a pencil out of the table drawer and wrote it down.

I sat staring at that piece of paper and trying to decide what I'd say if I got up my nerve to say anything and suddenly, almost without thinking about it, I started punching in the numbers. The phone rang twice and a man answered.

"Hi, this is Dave. How can I help you?" he said, and his voice was warm and soft and sounded like maybe he'd known me forever and was really glad to hear from me today.

I took a deep breath and held tight to the phone until my fingers hurt. But the words wouldn't come. They sat there, just inside my head, waiting for me to tell

Dave how sometimes I was scared about my mother and thought maybe it was my fault, the way she was. How I was afraid to drive with her and could mostly always tell when she'd had too much to drink because of the way her hands shook and she talked funny and made me not like her. And how I got mad at her and at my dad and at myself, for feeling the way I did, and sometimes wanted to smash things.

"It's okay," said Dave. "Take your time."

But the words still wouldn't come. And then I thought what if he has Caller ID. What if he knows my number and calls back or maybe even gets our name from the phone company and calls my mother or my father and wants to know what I'm doing calling the HELPline.

"Sometimes it's hard to get started," said Dave. "So maybe we could just talk about—"

And I hung up the phone.

I was sitting on my mother's bed, thinking about Dave and how maybe, someday, I'd be brave enough to call him again, when the phone rang and I grabbed for it, before I could think not to answer.

"Hello," I said, trying at the last minute to sound deep and rumbly.

"Hannah, is that you?" my mother asked. "What's wrong with your voice?"

"My strep throat, I guess," I said, coughing a couple of times.

"How are you feeling?" she asked.

"Good, better. It's just that I haven't been using my voice is all." And I held the receiver with my shoulder and tore the piece of paper with Dave's number on it into about a million pieces.

"Well, that's good," said Mom. "Because I'm going to be longer than I thought. The retiree wants her picture taken with just about everyone she's ever known —and that has to be done after the luncheon. And then one of the women here wants to get together for a drink and talk about a project she has in mind. So if you're sure you'll be all right . . ."

"I'm fine, Mom," I said, but what I wanted to say was *Don't have a drink with that lady. Don't have any drinks at all and just take your pictures and come home.*

"Have you had your lunch?" my mother went on. "And taken your medicine?"

"Yes, and no. But I will now, take my medicine, I mean."

And I did. After we hung up I went downstairs and took it and ate some more cold spaghetti. Then I went to stand at the front window again, only this time there wasn't even Mrs. Miller and her sausage dog to look at. I felt like maybe I was going to explode, like the house wasn't big enough to hold me.

I wanted to call Dave—but I knew I wouldn't. I wanted to call my father and tell him to come home from work, that there was something wrong with Mom and what could we do about it. Only Dad didn't know there was anything wrong—or if he did, he didn't let on. Which is sometimes sort of as bad as not knowing something. I wanted to call Granddad and say if he could write all those columns, then why couldn't he think of something to do about my mother. I wanted to call Gloria and Sam and Ms. Garcia at school, and maybe even Dr. Kelly again. I wanted, I wanted, I wanted. And suddenly I yelled out *HELP* right there in the middle-of-the-day quiet of that empty house.

I went upstairs and started pulling off my pajamas and putting on my clothes, almost without thinking about it. I grabbed my library card and brushed my hair and went downstairs and put on my coat and found my key and wrapped a scarf around my neck. And all the way to the library I thought of what I'd say if anybody asked me why I was there. "A school project," I said out loud, practicing how I'd tell the librarian that some of us were working on AIDS and drugs and acid rain and saving the whales. And how my topic was alcoholism. And if she asked what I was doing there in the middle of a school day, I'd just tell the truth and say how I'd been sick but now I was better and thought I'd get an early start.

Except all of a sudden I didn't feel better. I swallowed carefully and my throat hurt more than I thought it would and when I got to the library it was hot and steamy inside and the walls seemed to sway and push closer than they ought to. I used the microfiche, squinting into the machine and writing down a bunch of titles and call numbers on a scrap of paper, then afterward just standing there and looking at them. The thing is that I'm not always very good at finding books in the library, at least not books with numbers on them, and mostly I just ask the librarian. But today I didn't. Today I just figured it out for myself, going up one aisle and down another.

I got lost once and ended up in "Mysteries." Then I found the 500s and went along the shelves till I came to the 300s and some of the numbers that matched the numbers on my piece of paper. I took the books down and looked at them and put them in a pile to take with me.

I checked them out and started home, and when I was halfway there I stopped, right in the middle of the sidewalk, and stood thinking about what I'd do if Mom found them, or even Dad. And then I turned and went back to the library, pushing the books into the outside drop and hearing them thud, thud, thud as they hit the bottom.

When I got home I threw my coat in the closet and went upstairs and climbed in bed, with the rest of my clothes still on. And I slept. The next thing I knew, the room was kind of shadowy and I could hear my father, downstairs, calling me.

"Hannah, Hannah? Where are you?" He ran upstairs, flipping on lights along the way. "Where's your mother?" he said, coming in and turning the bedside table lamp on, so that a sort of rosy glow filled the room.

"Out to lunch," I said.

"Out to lunch?" said Dad. "It's after six. Have you heard from her at all?"

"Yeah," I said, sitting up and blinking and trying to get myself all the way awake. "She called—"

"When?"

"Around noon. I know 'cause it was after I ate my lunch and I ate my lunch really early and—"

"What did she say?"

"That she'd be late. That she had to take extra pictures and then there was this lady who wanted her to have a drink and talk about something. A project or something."

"A project?" said Dad, taking off his tie and rolling up his sleeves. "A drink?"

"Yeah, and I wanted to tell her not to have a drink with that lady because sometimes . . . because maybe . . . because, just because."

Dad turned and leaned against his dresser, resting his head on his arms. I looked at him and it was scary, sort of, to see him leaning on anything, 'cause it's Dad, mostly, who holds things up. And for a minute I thought we could talk, but then he swung around and said, "Don't worry about your mother, Hannah. I'm sure the time just got away from her and she'll be home any minute. Now, let's go downstairs and fix some supper, shall we?"

Dad made a salad and we ate the rest of the cold spaghetti, only heated now, in the microwave. Afterward we watched the news and "Jeopardy," except that Dad didn't call out the questions this time and the room seemed really quiet, and different. Then he went off to correct papers and I talked to Sam on the telephone and took a bubble bath and started a letter to Jessie Lee and went to bed.

It was ages later that I heard my mother come in, and suddenly it was as though I'd been holding my breath and I didn't have to hold it anymore. And I was sleepier than I'd ever been, in my whole entire life.

When I woke the next morning, Saturday, the sun

was shining and I could smell coffee and hear my father moving around in the kitchen.

"Your mother has a headache today, so we'll just let her sleep in," he said when I went downstairs.

And him saying it, and me watching myself, as if from far away, made it seem like a movie I'd seen before.

Nine

It all started on a Thursday night in November. Dad was correcting papers and I was doing my homework at the dining room table and Mom had just come up from working in her basement darkroom when the phone rang. I heard my mother answer it, heard her voice soft and musical before it turned shrill and then into an almost scream. After that she slammed the receiver against the wall and let it drop and dangle there on the cord until it started to make that squawking noise that phones make when you need to hang them up right.

Mom swung around and yanked a bottle out of the cupboard and poured a drink and added a little bit of water and stirred it with her finger and drank it almost before I had a chance to get up and go into the kitchen; before Dad had a chance to get down from the second floor.

"What's wrong?" I said.

"What's wrong?" said Dad, coming in behind me.

"Witch," said Mom. She turned back to the bottle and, without even trying to hide it, poured another drink.

"Who? Who's a witch?" said Dad. He took the bottle out of her hand and then stood for a minute, looking at it, before putting it on the counter.

"That woman."

"What woman?"

"You know, that Joan Calloway, the one I talked to at that retirement luncheon I did down at the Hyatt. She wanted me to do the photographs for a book she's doing on hidden gardens in Maryland—you know, not the big important ones, but the small tucked-away places—and I'd even started researching it and taken some fall shots, in case we wanted them for contrast, and—and—" She pushed away from the sink and circled the kitchen like a lion in the zoo.

"She wanted me to do the pictures—but now she doesn't. Now she's changed her mind. That's what she called to tell me. 'I've decided to go with someone else' is what she said. 'Someone who doesn't have such un —un—'" She stumbled over the word, shaking her head and rubbing her mouth. "'Such unresolved problems,'" Mom said all at once, then grabbed the vodka bottle again and tilted it into her glass, filling it to the brim.

"Undissolved problems are the best kind to have," she sort of sang, looking from Dad to me.

"Unresolved," I said, without knowing I was going to say it.

"What do you know about it?" Mom swung at me, shooting out her hand so that her drink splashed down my front and onto the floor.

"Nothing," I said. "It was just the word—'unresolved' instead of 'undissolved.'" I wanted to shut up, but my mouth kept going. "I didn't mean anything. I don't even know why I said it. It's just that—"

"Stop looking at me," my mother said. "Both of you stop looking at me." And she took her glass and ran out of the room and up the stairs. We heard her overhead, pacing through all of the second floor, and once Dad started after her, but when he got as far as the hall he turned and came back.

"I don't know," he said, shaking his head. "Maybe it'd be better—I just don't know."

"But I *want* you to know," I heard myself shout. "I want you to know what to do and then go *do* it."

Before I had a chance to say any more, Mom came down the steps and went out the front door, slamming it behind her. Dad and I got to the porch just in time to see her car pulling away from the curb. She tore up the street and screeched around the corner, and for ages afterward, in the quiet and the dark, it seemed as if I could hear my mother's car spinning crazily through the neighborhood, getting farther and farther away. "She's not supposed to drive," I said when I couldn't hear her anymore. "People like that are not *supposed* to drive."

"Your mother's upset right now, but she's sensible. She'll be careful," my father said, sort of sighing when he spoke.

"*No*," I cried, holding on to the word till I couldn't hold it anymore. "*No—no—no*. She's not upset, she's not sensible, she's not careful. She's *drunk*." And there, it was out—the word I'd hardly ever even dared think before.

"Hannah, Hannah," he said, reaching for me. But I pulled away and went into the house, hearing him come after me.

"She's, you know, what I said. And when she is, then she drives like crazy, and it makes me scared and I'm afraid she's going to crash and I don't want to be with her and I don't want her to be by herself and why don't you *do* something."

"Because I don't know what to do." My father spoke slowly as he sat on the edge of the couch, dropping his head into his hands. "Oh, God, I've tried. I've talked to doctors, to counselors, to anybody I thought might have the answer. I've talked to your mother until I can't talk anymore."

"But not to me. You didn't talk to me. *Never once*."

He got up and came toward me and put his hand on my head. "That's because I didn't want you to have to know."

"But I *did*."

"Yes, I guess you did," said Dad. "And I should've figured that you couldn't *not* know. It's just that I wanted you to—not to . . . I wanted you to be the one person who was spared from all this."

"Do other people know?" I asked.

He nodded. "Granddad's talked to me. He and Gloria've been worried about you, but I told them you didn't—" He shook his head before going on. "I guess I wanted it to be just *my* problem. Mine and your mother's."

"What about Mom?" I said. "Why doesn't she *stop*?"

"She has to *want* to," said Dad. "Your mother has to be the one who—"

I put my hands up over my ears and pulled away from him. I ran into the kitchen and took the bottle off the counter and opened it and poured what was inside down the drain. The bottle was plastic, and when it was empty I beat it against the counter. Beat and beat and beat until it was dented and sort of smashed. My father came in behind me and took hold of my shoulders while I kept on beating until my arm hurt and I couldn't do it anymore. Then I turned and fell against him and he held me tight.

"Sometimes I thought I was the only one who knew," I said into his shirt. "And like there was this big cage that'd come down around me, trapping me, sort of."

"I hope it's a big one, Hannah, because we're in it together," said Dad.

And it was weird. I mean, nothing had *really* changed, but in a way everything had.

When I came into the kitchen the next morning, Dad was still in his clothes from the night before, and I was pretty sure he hadn't been to bed. He was talking on the phone, arranging for a substitute to take his classes, and when he hung up I said, "Aren't you going to work today?"

"Well, no. I think I'd better hang around here, for when your mother gets home," he said. And all of a sudden I felt like I did when I was a kid and was playing with bubbles—and the bubbles burst. I mean, the whole time I'd been getting dressed I hadn't looked out the window to see if her car was home. On purpose. I'd tiptoed past the door of her room and hadn't even peeked in. On purpose. And I hadn't called out to her either. On purpose. That way, I told myself, when I got downstairs Mom'd be sure to be there, packing my lunch at the kitchen counter, or pouring herself a cup of coffee. But she wasn't. And I could tell, by the ragged look on Dad's face, that he hadn't heard from her either.

"She didn't call?" I asked.

"No, but she'll be home today, just you wait and see," he said in that kind of voice that people use when they don't actually believe what they're saying. "Now, have some breakfast and get along to school. Today's your big day, isn't it? Or, I guess, tonight's your big night, with the Fall Fling and you and your friends dancing to the *Hungarian Rhapsody*. And we'll all be there, including your mom."

"I could stay home," I said. "From school, I mean."

"What?" said Dad. "And have you miss that one last rehearsal? Gypsy dancers need practice, everybody knows that." He snapped his fingers, as though they were castanets, and spun around in a circle right there in the middle of the kitchen. And the really strange thing was that Dad trying so hard and all made me feel sad instead of happy.

Just before school was out that afternoon, Mrs. Valenti, the principal, came on the loudspeaker and said, "Don't worry, girls and boys—a poor dress rehearsal always makes for a good performance." I guess that tells something about the kind of practice we had. All the gypsy dancers (Sam and Effie and Rosa and I) really messed up and Stevie Reilly, who was reciting a big long poem called "The Highwayman," forgot the whole middle chunk; the violin players sounded squeaky and the tumblers fell sideways doing their backwards rolls.

Then Mrs. Valenti went on to say, "And remember, I want each and every performer to rest this afternoon. Rest, rest, rest, so you won't come in here all tired out tonight. So you'll do your families and friends *proud*. Now, break a leg, everybody."

"Is Mom here yet?" I asked my father as soon as I got home.

"No," he said. "But she called. She's in Virginia, visiting some friends, and she sounded good. Fine. Fine." And just the way he wasn't exactly looking at me when he was talking made me pretty sure my mother hadn't called, and that my father was lying.

And then about a million feelings bunched up inside my head. I mean, ever since I can remember, my parents had told me lying was wrong—only now we were all doing it. Because of Mom. And suddenly it was like we were back to the same old game, and we were playing by the same old rules.

"She didn't call, did she?" I asked.

"She didn't call," said Dad. "But she will. I'm sure of it."

Just then the phone rang and it was Sam to see if I wanted to come over there and get ready for the show. "We can rest, the way Mrs. Valenti said to do, and then my mom'll fix us something to eat so we can get up to school early," she said.

I told her yes, and after we hung up I took a shower and washed my hair. Afterward, when I got to Sam's, we mostly just lay on the twin beds in her room with damp washcloths on our eyes (to make them sparkle) and talked about how maybe we'd be *real* stars someday, except that I planned to be a writer and Sam wanted to be a blacksmith, or else a veterinarian. We talked about a bunch of other stuff, too: like how the eighth-grade boys were cuter than the seventh-grade boys and would Stevie Reilly make it all the way through "The Highwayman" this time and what we were going to do on our Thanksgiving vacation. I even told Sam that Mom probably wouldn't be coming to the show, because she was in Virginia, and then I felt bad for saying what I did except the weird thing was that once I'd said the words out loud it made it seem that Mom really was someplace. And not just gone.

Sam's mother served us chicken à la king on waffles at the kitchen table and told her brothers not to bug us, that we were superstars, and then we put on our costumes and her father drove us to school.

When the show began, Sam and Effie and Rosa and I sat backstage and listened to Stevie Reilly say his whole poem without any mistakes, and the violins not squeak, and the rest of the acts sound the way they were supposed to sound. And then, all of a sudden, it was our turn and we were up on the stage and the music teacher put the tape on and the curtain opened and we began. From the very start, even when we were spinning around and stamping our feet and clacking our castanets, I kept thinking about my mom: how maybe she was really out there in the audience, standing in a doorway or sitting in the back. How maybe she was okay now and had driven from wherever she was, just to get here on time. But afterward, when we were all having punch and cookies in the cafeteria, I couldn't find her.

Dad was there, though, and Gloria and Granddad, and they kept hugging me and kissing me and telling me that their truthful and unbiased opinion was that the gypsy dancers were the best part of the show. And the whole time they were doing this there was a little scratchy thought, way down at the bottom of my mind: that maybe Mom would never come home and life would be simpler and I'd never be embarrassed again. Then a big wet guilt feeling settled over me and the cookie I was eating tasted like cardboard and I whispered under my breath that I didn't mean it. Not a word of it.

Ten

Saturday took forever, and so did Sunday. Pretty much what we did was wait for the phone to ring and in between times Dad called around to hospitals and even to the state police, asking if there had been an accident. That was when I went out, to the pay phone across from the library, and called the HELPline. Instead of Dave, someone named Marilyn answered, and at first I was mad, like maybe he'd deserted me, only she sounded really nice and when she asked how she could help I told her about Mom walking out one night, slamming the door behind her, and how Dad and I were really worried, especially because she'd been drinking. And besides that, she hadn't taken a suitcase.

The more I talked, the more my voice started to shake, and I guess Marilyn could hear it because she said she knew this was really hard but not to hang up and maybe we could sort it all out and how I had to remember that none of this was my fault. But I did, hang up, I mean. After that I told the story about a trillion times, inside my head, till I was sure the words had worn ruts in my brain. Then I just walked, for ages, kicking at leaves and thinking how maybe what I'd do was go home and tell Dad about Dave and Marilyn and the HELPline. And how together we would call them back.

When I got home, though, Mr. Porter from next door was there, borrowing a screwdriver, and he stayed for ages, and then after he left, Dad ran out to get a pizza. While he was gone I set the table and made a salad and after he got back we sort of ate. But mostly we didn't. Mostly we just pushed the food around our plates and *pretended* to eat.

"Dad," I said, poking at a piece of cheese that was beginning to look like plastic, "there's this number I found, in the phone book, and it's for something called the HELPline, and it's for people like Mom. And I thought maybe we could call them and they'd tell us what to do and if we don't there's this place Miss Duncan told us about in health class that's just for the families. You know, the *families* of people like Mom."

"Not now, Hannah," said Dad. "It's your mother we're concerned about here. It's your *mother* we have to find. Your mother—"

"It's us, too." And when I said the words they sounded small and far away.

"Not now." My father slammed his hand down flat on the table, so that the dishes jumped. "For God's sake, not *now*." He got up, toppling his chair, and went to stand by the sink, staring out into the dark. The room was quiet, except for the hum of the refrigerator, and I sat there, because I didn't know what else to do. Sat there and ran the pizza cutter back and forth on the cardboard box.

"I'm sorry, Hannah." Dad picked up his chair and came to sit beside me. "But this whole thing is making me crazy. And afterward, when your mother's home and things are okay, then we *will* call one of those places. Because you're right—it is about us, too."

My eyes filled with tears, partly, I guess, on account of the way Dad had yelled, and partly on account of the way he'd said he was sorry. I chewed on a piece of pizza and willed myself not to cry.

All of a sudden we heard Mom come in, and then she was there, at the kitchen door, still in the same clothes she'd had on when she left, only now they were gross and dirty and smelled of throw-up. She stood for a minute before moving into the room and dropping her car keys on the table. She turned and went out into the hall and up the stairs, still without saying anything. Dad hurried after her, and in a few minutes I heard the shower running upstairs, and a few minutes after that he was back carrying her clothes all bunched up in his arms. I watched from the door as he went outside and shoved them way deep into the garbage can.

"Do you mind cleaning up down here?" he said when

he came in. "I want to help your mother into bed—but she's fine, Hannah. What she needs now is a good night's sleep."

The next few days, Mom really was fine. I mean, she was quiet and not like herself at all and she never once told us where she'd been, but she wasn't drinking. At least, I don't think she was. I looked in the cupboard a couple of times, but I didn't see any vodka, and I didn't look any further. Mostly, I guess, 'cause I didn't want to know.

The day before Thanksgiving she made a pumpkin pie and an apple pie and the next day we took them to Columbia, to Aunt Pauli and Uncle Bill's for dinner. And the thing was that everybody told her about a million times how good they were and it was almost like they were being *careful* with her. Which made me think they all knew what had happened. And I didn't know whether they knew because Dad had told them, or just because they *knew*, the way people sometimes do, about other people they care about.

After the dishes were done we all sat around the dining room table and played Trivial Pursuit, the Vintage Years version, and Granddad knew more answers than anybody, except he said that was because he'd lived the longest. I didn't know *anything*, and my cousin Casey wasn't much better, so the two of us gave up and wandered into the family room. He was kneeling on the floor, putting a movie in the VCR, when he said, "Things okay, Hannah? At home, I mean. Because if you ever need to talk, just give a holler."

I stood looking down at him and for a minute I

wanted to blab it all: about Mom and how she'd gone off somewhere only now she was home and how, more than anything, I wanted for her never to drink another drink. Instead I just sighed and shrugged and said, "Oh, well, everything's fine."

When we left Aunt Pauli's I was so stuffed I swore I'd never eat again, but by the time we got home and I went to bed and read three chapters of my book I was wide awake and starving. I got up and tiptoed down the steps so I wouldn't disturb my parents, but when I got to the bottom I saw a light in the sun porch. Mom was sitting on the couch in her rose-colored robe looking sort of mellow. Even though the TV was on she didn't seem to be watching it, and when she heard me come in she looked up and smiled and patted the seat next to her.

"Can't you sleep either, Hannah-banana?" she said.

"Well, I was hungry—or thirsty—but then I saw the light and—"

"Do you want some milk?" Mom asked. But by then I was curled up next to her, with my head in her lap, and she was rubbing my back . . . the way she always used to do when I was little.

"No, not now," I said. And for a while after that we sat without saying anything. The television droned and the pipes in the wall made a crackling noise.

"Did you have a good time tonight?" she asked.

"Yes," I said. I felt sleepy and sort of like I was floating. "I like it when you're like this."

"Like what?"

"Oh, you know, sort of soft and all. I like it when

you're not drinking, and when you do I get scared."

"*Drinking?*" I felt her body stiffen and she pulled away and went to stand by the window. "Drinking? What's the big deal about drinking? Everybody takes a drink—your father and your grandfather and Gloria, Bill, Pauli. Everybody I *know.*"

"But, Mom—" I struggled to sit up, wanting her to come back or for me to go to her.

"But, Mom what? You started this."

"It's just that, sometimes, like the other day when you went away and then we didn't know where you were and Dad was really worried, and so was I and—"

"I guess you had a fine time talking about me, didn't you? Is that what you and your father do, when I'm not here, or even when I am? Talk about me like that. Talk, talk, talk. They were all watching me tonight, don't think I couldn't see it. Waiting for me to explode. Waiting so they could lecture me again. Your father and your grandfather. Try to get me to straighten up."

She turned to face me, standing as tall as she could, and moved closer. "Well, let me tell you one thing. Sure I take a drink from time to time, everybody does, and you probably will, too, when you're older."

"No," I said. "I never will."

"But I know exactly what I'm doing and it's not a problem for me. No matter what you and your father say. No matter what *anybody* says." She swooped down and picked up a glass off the floor, then turned and walked carefully out of the room, steadying herself on the doorframe as she went. And from the kitchen I heard the clatter of ice cubes before I ran upstairs and shut my door.

Eleven

"Your Mom and Dad'd let you, Hannah. Why don't you just *ask* them," said Sam.

"Come on," said Effie.

"Pleeee-ease," said Rosa. "Otherwise we'll have *nothing* to do during all of vacation."

"They wouldn't," I said, crossing my fingers under the table. I picked up my fork and poked at the goop the cafeteria lady had plopped down on my plate. "Okay, everybody gets one guess. What's the mystery meal today?"

"She's changing the subject," said Effie.

"And you were our only *hope*," said Rosa.

"I'll ask your mom," said Sam. "We'll go to your house after school and if she's home she'll probably tell us to go get something to eat and then while we're eating she'll make conversation, the way mothers do, and when she says, 'Well, Sam, what big plans do you have for your Christmas vacation?' that's when I'll wail and say, 'Oh, Mrs. Brant, there's nothing *to* do and we need to have a party but there's no place to have it and —and—'"

"No," I said, the word coming out louder than I'd meant for it to. "You don't understand. My parents think you have to be practically ancient to have a boy-girl party and even last year when we went to that one at Emily's they both just sighed and rolled their eyes a whole bunch."

"They're all alike," said Effie. "Parents, I mean."

"And my mother says she's had enough parties with my older sisters and now's her turn to get a break and she doesn't have to start over again with me," said Sam.

"And mine says all *that*, plus my great-aunt's coming for the holidays and whenever she's there Mom's forever going around saying 'Shhhhh.' So forget a party," said Rosa.

"Yeah," said Effie and Sam together.

I breathed a giant sigh of relief and even ate some of the mystery meal before I caught myself. I mean, it was true about my parents thinking I was too young for a boy-girl party, but what if Sam really did ask Mom and what if she said yes and then I ended up having a party, and people came, and what if Mom hung around and she maybe had too much to drink and fell into something or broke something or spilled something, or even went to sleep on the couch? *What if?* I got cold and clammy just thinking about it.

"Maybe someone else will," Sam was saying when I tuned back in.

"Will what?" I said.

"Have a party."

"Yeah. I guess. Maybe."

I thought about it in the next class, which was health. How maybe there *wouldn't* be anything to do during the Christmas vacation and even if I sat home all day every day and all night every night I still couldn't ask my parents to let me have a party. I thought about Christmas shopping and how I didn't have very much money and how Mom and Dad would probably give me jobs around the house that didn't really need doing— and pay me for them, the same as they did every year. I thought how there was a lot to worry about with Christmas and how, maybe, it was better when I was younger and Santa Claus came and that was it.

And, mostly, I thought about Mom, and how holidays weren't usually very good for her and how I ended up keeping my fingers crossed during the whole entire time. Well, not really crossed but with that fingers-crossed feeling.

Except that this year Christmas went along pretty well. Mom was really busy beforehand because of people wanting pictures of their kids and grandkids, the kind of stuff she hates doing but does anyway—for money. And then there was this woman author who needed a picture for a book jacket and had Mom take about a jillion shots before she ended up choosing one. But when she came to pick the pictures up she brought a case of wine. Mom opened it right then and took out one of the bottles and stood cradling it in her arms and sort of stroking it, like maybe it was a baby or something.

Afterward she carried the case downstairs and stored it in the far back corner of her darkroom. And the weird thing was that that night at supper, when the three of us tell each other the stuff that went on during the day, Mom never mentioned it. And the *weirder* thing was that I didn't either. Mostly, I guess, 'cause I could tell that Dad thought that Mom was doing better. And so did I. Or, more than anything, I *wanted* to think so.

What I did do, though, was sneak down into her darkroom every couple of days, when Mom wasn't there, and open up that case of wine and count the bottles as they went from twelve to eleven to ten to nine to eight to seven to six to five to four to three to two to one to none. All the way down.

But in spite of the woman author and the wine and the disappearing bottles, it was still a pretty good Christmas. I mean, once Dad was out of school he sort of took charge, the way he does every year. That's because, in our family, Dad's the one who really gets into Christmas. Mom's idea, when she's not working, is to curl up on her favorite end of the couch and listen to carols on the CD player and read *A Child's Christmas in Wales* aloud, even if there's no one there to listen. Either that or watch *White Christmas*, which we all do every year sometime in December, and then, when it's done, Mom and I sing all the songs and do the sisters act and Dad holds his ears and pretends he doesn't like it —but he does.

Anyway, Dad made the wreath for the front door, and the back door, too. He lined the mantel with holly and put the manger set in front of it and stood holding a shepherd with a broken leg and said, the way he does every year, "I remember this from when *I* was a kid." Then, the Saturday before Christmas, the three of us went out to get the tree.

"We'll get a perfect one this year," said Mom, shaping a tree in the air with her hands. "With branches that are full and no bare spots and a place on top for the angel."

We didn't, though. We got the kind I talk my parents into every time—tall and skinny and spindly, with an empty sort of hole in back where there aren't any branches. That's because whenever we go Christmas-tree shopping there's always one that I know, sure as anything, won't get taken home by anybody. Unless we take it.

"A Charlie Brown tree," said Mom, same as she says every year.

"It'll be a challenge," said Dad, same as *he* says every year.

He tied it to the roof of the car and we took it home and put it, bare side facing the wall, in a corner of the living room. We hung tiny white lights on it, and about a million ornaments and icicles from the tip of every branch. Then we stood and looked at it and said, "This is the best tree we've ever had." Same as we say every year.

Another good thing that happened before Christmas

was that I got cards in the mail from Mandy, Sue, and Jessie Lee and across the bottom of hers Jessie Lee wrote *Almost summer*. It wasn't really, but I closed my eyes and pretended and thought how, after the holidays and after we went back to school and maybe after Valentine's Day, it nearly would be.

I wanted a puppy for Christmas but I got a camera. I wasn't surprised, about the puppy, I mean, because one of the mother things my mom's always told me is about the time when she was little and had a dog and how the dog got loose and ran in front of a car and was killed right while she was watching. And how she'd never, ever, take the chance of that happening again. But the camera was nice, anyway, and I also got about a ton of film to go with it, a photo album, a funky black sweater (even though Mom hates black), two pairs of earrings, and three paperbacks.

After we'd gone to church and opened our presents and sat around for the boring middle part of Christmas, we went to Granddad and Gloria's for this humongous turkey dinner. Aunt Pauli, Uncle Bill, and Casey were there, too, and so was Helene, who's Granddad's sister and my great-aunt except she doesn't like to be called "Aunt," and who's small like a bird and wears spiky high heels and clothes with sequins. And the really neat part is that for days after she's been someplace, people are forever finding sequins under cushions and in the carpet, and once, even, in the dishwasher.

Casey left early, on a date, and when the dishes were done I sat by the fire in the living room, listening to the grownups talk about politics, and feeling happy and full. And forgetting to worry about Mom for a while.

Twelve

Nobody had a party during the holidays, at least nobody in the entire seventh grade that I heard about, and my friends and I pretty much just hung out. At the mall, some, or at Effie's, but mostly at Sam's because there're so many kids there all the time that her mother never seems to mind a few more. On New Year's Eve afternoon, though, Sam was at my house and we were upstairs making our New Year's resolutions. Not the gross kind, like studying harder, but a whole bunch that had to do with boys and how we looked and, even, developing a deep and mysterious personality. It'd been snowing when Sam got here, but between then and when we looked up from making our lists it was as if somebody had dumped about a ton of snow on the world around us.

We ran downstairs and were standing at the front door, staring out and eating the broken pieces of ginger Christmas cookies that were all that was left in the bottom of the tin, when Mom pulled into the driveway.

She stopped for a minute to talk to Mrs. Porter from next door and then came in, stamping her feet and shaking the snow out of her hair. "That's some fierce storm out there," she said. "Kay Porter just told me that there've already been all kinds of cancellations on the radio. *And* she and Bob are having a neighborhood snow party tonight."

"What's a snow party?" I asked.

"Oh, you know, a spur-of-the-moment party, because of the snow, and where everybody can walk to get there. I don't think anybody'll want to be out driving in this."

We followed Mom into the kitchen and watched as she emptied her grocery bag onto the table. "What's that for?" I said, pointing to a package of ground beef.

"Meat loaf, for supper," she said.

"Meat loaf? I thought we were having lasagna. I saw you making it this morning."

"Yes, but that was for *tomorrow*, when the family's here. I figure that by now everybody's ham-and-tur-keyed out. And tonight it's meat loaf," said Mom as she dumped the beef into a bowl and added eggs and bread crumbs and a lot of other stuff.

"Say, I've got an idea," she said, looking up from mushing the meat loaf gunk with her hands. "Sam, why don't you stay for supper and then spend the night here with Hannah? You can have your own private New Year's Eve party while we're next door."

"I could," said Sam.

"She couldn't," I said at exactly the same time.

"Why on earth not?" said Mom, looking at me and squinting her eyes, the way she does when she thinks I've said something I shouldn't't've.

"Because her mother wouldn't know where she was," I said.

"She'll telephone," said Mom.

"I'll telephone," said Sam.

"And besides, she doesn't have any pajamas. Or toothbrush, either," I said.

"Hannah," said Mom, really squinting at me this time. "You have an extra flannel nightgown and I even have a brand-new never-out-of-the-box toothbrush upstairs. Now, go on, Sam. Call."

"Should I?" said Sam, looking at me and sort of waiting.

And in that waiting time I thought how I really wanted Sam to sleep over, the way she used to, and wondered if Mom'd be okay and if I dared take the chance.

"Yeah, call," I said, after a deep breath. "Go ahead and call."

We all ate supper from trays in the sun porch, with the light down low and the curtains open wide, so we could watch the snow piling up on three sides around us. Every once in a while one or the other of us would get up and peer out the window at a spot just below the streetlamp, to see if it was still coming down. Before we ate, Mom brought in wine for her and Dad and ginger ale in fancy glasses for Sam and me, which I thought was really queer and juvenile and the kind of thing you do for little kids.

"How queer," I whispered to Sam, under my breath.

"I think it's nice," Sam whispered back, which is easy to say when it's someone else's parents who are being queer and juvenile.

"A toast," said Mom, holding out her glass and waiting for Dad and Sam and me to do the same thing. I caught my breath and pinched myself hard on the side of the leg, but Mom's voice, when she spoke, was soft and clear, and all she said was "To the New Year."

"Hear! Hear!" said Dad.

"Hear! Hear!" said Sam and I.

After my parents had gone next door, Sam and I watched an old movie called *Auntie Mame*. We made popcorn and talked to Effie, and Rosa, then Effie again, on the telephone. We gathered up a bunch of pots and pans from the kitchen and watched the countdown from Times Square in New York City on TV, waiting for it to be twelve o'clock. And right at midnight we went out onto the porch and banged and clattered our pots and pans. Then, as if we'd both together had the same idea, we ran down into the front yard, flopping over backwards and making angels in the snow.

Later, when we were in bed, we lay there, whispering back and forth and watching the corners of the room and the way the snow outside made them almost as bright as day. Sam was in the middle of telling me about her sister Leslie and this boy who really likes her and how he calls every night at 7:05 and how Leslie pitches an absolute fit if anyone else in the family is anywhere *near* the phone, when we heard the sound of the party breaking up next door.

"Happy New Year," the voices called. "Happy New Year."

"Thank you . . . See you . . . Good night . . ."

Next we heard my mother and father stomping the snow off their boots and coming in the front door. "So long, it's been good to know yuh," my mother sang, her voice sounding harsh and croaky and filling all the spaces of the house. "So long, it's been good to know yuh . . ."

She started up the stairs, then stopped and went back, sort of all in a thud. She started up a second time and I heard her slam against the wall, heard my father calling to her, telling her to wait.

"So long, it's been good to know yuh," she sang and I heard her put her feet down heavily on one step, and another, and another.

"Quick," I said, leaning across the space between the two beds and pulling at Sam's covers. "Pretend you're asleep."

Mom was at the top of the stairs. I crossed my fingers and prayed for her not to fall.

"So long," she sang again. "So long . . ."

I heard her move away from the stairs and start along the hall; heard her stop outside my room, heard her throw my door open wide so that it slammed against the wall. Then she spun into the room. I watched her through half-shut eyes as she stood swaying there, still in her winter coat, and sending out patches of freezing air.

"Shhhhh," she said in a booming voice. "So long, it's been good to know yuh . . ." She sang the words of the song slowly, dragging them out, before turning and lunging into the space between the beds. She leaned low over Sam, staring at her, and I hardly dared breathe and held myself straight and dug my fingers into the blanket.

"Oh, yes, Sam," my mother said before she swung around to my bed and threw herself across it, pinning me down, coughing, and saying, "And Hannah-banana." Her spit stung my face and I groaned in pretend sleep.

Then my father was there, pulling at her arm and hoisting her up. He was steering her toward the door when she broke away from him and lurched back into the room. She crashed into the table and sent the dollhouse sliding onto the floor. Dad caught hold of her again, pushing her out into the hall and pulling the door shut behind him.

I knew that Sam was awake, but she didn't speak and I didn't speak. We both just lay there, stiff and still. And ages later, after I was sure that she was asleep, I got out of bed and picked up the dollhouse, feeling all over to see if it was broken, and set it back on the table.

When I woke the next morning, Sam was already up and dressed. "I've got to be home early," she said.

"And not stay for pancakes?" I said. "We pretty

much always have pancakes on holidays, and sometimes on Sundays too.''

''But my mother said—yesterday, when I called her.''

''Yeah—well—okay.'' And the whole time we were talking we looked away from each other.

I went downstairs with Sam and put my boots on over my bare feet and my ski jacket over my nightgown and followed her outside and off the porch and along the walk partway, smooshing the footprints my mother and father had made coming home the night before.

''Well, thanks,'' she said.

''Yeah, see you,'' I said.

I stood and watched as Sam made her way through the snow still heaped on the sidewalks, wondering all the while if she'd turn and wave when she got to the corner, the way she always does. She did, and I waved back, and I suddenly wanted to run after her, fighting the drifts, telling her how my mom wasn't like that all the time and how much I hated it and wanted to do something about it but didn't know what or how. I stood where I was, though, until it was too cold to stand there any longer, and when I turned to go back inside, Mr. Porter was just coming out of the house next door with his dog. ''Happy New Year, Hannah,'' he called. ''Your mother certainly was the life of the party last night. Yes ma'am. The life of the party.''

I said before how there was a boring chunk right in the middle of Christmas Day. Well, New Year's Day is mostly boring all the way through. Dad called early to tell Gloria and Granddad and Aunt Pauli and Uncle Bill that Mom was sick with the stomach flu, and for them not to come. Mom pretty much stayed in bed except when she was spooking around the house and not saying anything. A couple of times I thought sure that Dad was going to talk about last night, but he didn't, and after a while I went upstairs to my room.

I checked the dollhouse again and arranged the furniture the way it was supposed to be. I stood looking at the house for a long time, wishing that I was small enough to crawl inside where it looked warm and comfortable and wonderfully safe.

Thirteen

I hadn't seen Sam for a couple of days and when we went back to school after New Year's I was sort of afraid *to* see her. I mean, would she say anything about the other night, and if she did, what would *I* say to her? Had she told Rosa, or Effie, or maybe her mother, and what if her mother said she couldn't stay overnight at my house ever again? Then I remembered that I didn't want her to stay overnight anyway—but even that didn't make me feel better.

All morning I was doing what Gloria calls "walking on eggs," and when we got to the cafeteria and were halfway through our pizza, Rosa looked over at me and said, "What's the matter with you, Hannah? You're acting weird." That's when Sam punched me on the arm, the way she does sometimes to show me things are okay, and said, "It's being back at school is all. Doesn't that make *you* feel weird? It does me." Then we all started twitching and rolling our eyes and I got out my Christmas camera and took a bunch of pictures and thought how I'd put them in my album under the heading "The Weird Ones."

On the way home, Sam and I took some more pictures, mostly of the leftover snow and a lopsided snowperson. Then we went to her house for cocoa. We were in the family room and Sam was setting up the Monopoly game and I was thinking how it was all a horrible mistake and I was really meant to be in a family like Sam's and how, probably, just after I was born and still in the hospital, some nurse had given me to the wrong family, when Mrs. Sardo came in and said, "Does your mother know where you are, Hannah?"

Now, it's my *personal opinion* that, as old as I am, I ought to be able to go someplace or not go someplace after school without forever having to check in at home. The trouble is that Mom and Dad (and most of my friends' parents) don't agree and they're always talking about "the way the world is today." Anyway, I groaned and got up and went to call.

The phone rang for ages and Mom's voice, when she answered it, sounded slurred and far away.

"Hi, Mom, it's me," I said. "Did I wake you or something?"

"Nooooo," said Mom, dragging the word out longer than it should've been.

"Were you working?"

"I'm working," she said after a while, "but I'm not *working*." And because I've heard her say this about a million times, I knew she meant she was doing something that was work but not her *real* work, which means her photography.

"Oh," I said. "Well, I'm at Sam's, if that's okay?"

For a long time after that she didn't say anything and it was as if she had drifted away from the phone, except that I could still hear her breathing.

"Mom, is it okay that I'm at Sam's and I'll be home after a while?" I said again.

"Yes," my mother said and she put the phone down, only she didn't put it on its other half but on the table or the floor or someplace because even though she was gone I could still hear her, running water and opening and closing the refrigerator. I stood for a minute, looking at the receiver in my hand and thinking how I probably should go home—except I didn't want to. I wanted to stay at Sam's and finish my cocoa and play Monopoly and not think about what was happening with my mother.

"She says okay," I said when I went back to the family room and we started our game. The trouble was I couldn't concentrate. I kept hearing Mom's voice inside my head and knowing that something wasn't right. And even though I was winning and had just put hotels on Boardwalk and Park Place, I bunched up my money and held it out to Sam. "I gotta go," I said.

"But she said 'okay,' " said Sam.

"Yeah, only I don't think she meant it."

"Oh, I get it," said Sam. "The kind of okay that *says*

stay but *means* 'If you know what's good for you you'll come home right away.' "

"Yeah," I said, snapping a rubber band around the property cards.

Mom was sitting halfway up on a ladder in the middle of the living room, drinking a glass of orange juice. And everything around her was a mess. There were Christmas tree ornaments all over the tabletops, the chairs, the sofa, and even a few crushed into the rug. Candy canes were thrown every which way, and the strings of lights were tangled half on and half off the tree. The manger was lying facedown on the floor with the shepherds and Wise Men scattered around it and the holly from the mantel in a heap on top.

"Mom, what're you doing?" I said, taking off my coat and holding it tight against me.

"Detrimming the tree," she said carefully.

"But why? It's not even Little Christmas yet, and anyway, Dad said we'd do it over the weekend."

"Ye—es, but I want it done *now*," she said, moving down a rung on the ladder and finally settling onto the floor.

I stood looking at the glass in my mother's hand, positive that it wasn't just orange juice, and thinking how it really wasn't unusual for her to decide to take the tree down. But the thing was that every other year she just did it—zap—like that. I mean, she brought the boxes up from the cellar, wrapped every ornament as she took it off, rolled each string of lights, packed away the manger, with Jesus and Mary and all the rest wrapped in tissue paper and tucked inside. Then she dragged the tree out the front door, vacuumed the rug, moved the furniture back, and she was done.

"What're you staring at?" she said.

"Nothing," I said. "It's just that maybe I could help. I'll get the boxes from the basement."

When I came back with the boxes, Mom was on the top of the ladder. She had latched onto the shepherd with the damaged leg and was holding it up to the light. "Broken," she said, snapping it in two and flipping it into the air with her finger.

"Mom, don't," I said, picking up the pieces and storing them away in a desk drawer. "That's really old— maybe even an heirloom."

"*Hair*loom, *hair*loom," she sang, swaying from side to side on the ladder till I thought that at any minute she would come crashing down. But I knew, sure as anything, that if I asked her to stop she'd just sway faster.

"I've got an idea," I said, holding tight to the ladder and trying to look like I wasn't. "How about I finish up here while you go on and start dinner." Mom thought about it for a minute, then climbed off the ladder, picked up her glass, and headed for the kitchen.

I dumped all the tissue paper out of the box and started to wrap, but I didn't get very far. I mean, every ornament had to be looked at because it told a story. There were bells that really rang and horns that tooted and birds with feathered tails that Granddad had when he was a boy. There was the coffee-can lid covered with blue yarn that I'd made in kindergarten and a miniature black running shoe that Mom had given Dad the year he took up jogging. There were tiny angels in silky dresses that a friend of Gloria's had made and a china Babar that Mom gave me once because Babar was one of my very favorite book characters.

When I finally looked up, there were tons of ornaments still to be wrapped—and I couldn't hear any dinner noises coming from the kitchen. I tiptoed through the dining room and peeked in, still holding tight to Babar. Mom was sitting at the kitchen table, stabbing at a dish of lasagna with a spoon, and there were tears running down her face. "What's wrong?" I asked.

" 'S frozen," she said. She turned her spoon around and dug at the lasagna with the handle, sending flecks of crystally tomato sauce out onto the table.

"Mom, don't," I said, grabbing for the dish. "This'll never thaw in time. We'll just have to eat something else, like eggs, or tuna."

"I'll *get* something." She jumped up, took her coat from the closet and her purse and car keys off the counter, and headed for the door—sort of like a tornado spinning through the room.

"Mom, wait. Don't go." I followed her through the house and onto the porch. "We'll find something here, like I said. Or maybe the lasagna's okay. Maybe we can thaw it in the microwave if we do it for a really long time."

"I *said* I'd get something." And she was gone, down the steps, slipping and sliding over icy patches on the walk, and pushing through a snowdrift in front of the curb. She struggled into the car and I ran after her, pounding on the rear window, calling, "Wait!"

She started the engine and in the beginning the

wheels spun and I crossed my fingers and prayed for her to be stuck. But she eased away from the curb and out to the middle of the street and I watched her go, listening to the tires crunch against the snow till she turned the corner.

When Dad came in sometime later he stood for a minute, looking at the mess in the living room. "Where's your mother?" he asked.

"At the store. But she shouldn't have gone," I said in a rush. "She was drinking orange juice that wasn't orange juice and acting funny and talking funny and—"

"Did she say where? Which store?"

"No. She just said the store, to get something for supper 'cause the lasagna was frozen hard."

He swung around and started for the door, then stopped and came back, pushing Christmas ornaments out of the way and sitting on the edge of the couch. "I'd go after her," he said. "I *want* to go after her, but I don't know which direction—which store." I sat on the floor next to him and picked strands of icicles off the rug and wound them around my finger till it was thick and silvery-looking, and throbbing inside. We stayed that way without saying anything and then Dad looked at me and shook his head slowly, like maybe he was just waking up, and said, "I've been kidding myself, Hannah. Kidding you and kidding myself. Hoping that things were getting better, even with what happened New Year's Eve."

"Me too," I said. "Even with the wine from the lady author."

"Wine?" said Dad. "What wine?"

I told him about the wine in the darkroom and the way the case kept getting emptier and emptier. After that we just sat there another whole long time. And when the phone rang, it was as though we'd been waiting for it all along.

I followed Dad into the kitchen and listened to his end of the conversation and mostly what he said was "Yes . . . Yes . . . Yes . . . I see . . ." It was when he said, "I'll be right there," that I knew, for sure, that something had happened to Mom.

"Your mother's had an accident and they've taken her to the emergency room at Union Memorial," he said after he had hung up. He was already reaching for his coat, looking around for his keys. "I've got to get right down there."

"What happened?" I said. "What happened to Mom?"

"They didn't say—just that there'd been an accident and that they were working on her."

I grabbed my ski jacket and started to put it on, but Dad took it away from me and dropped it on the table. "No, Hannah," he said, pulling me tight and holding me for a minute. "I want you to wait here."

"But, Dad—"

"Please—I don't know how long I'll be, or what I'll find when I get there."

I wanted to argue, but when I looked at him and saw the way his face was gray and shadowed I didn't. He turned to the phone, fumbling with the receiver and saying, "I'm going to call Gloria to come and wait with you."

When Gloria came to the door and rang the bell and I saw her there, I suddenly burst into tears. She took me into the living room and sat me on the cleared-off part of the couch and made a space for herself, all the time saying, "Now, now, now." I cried for ages and then I started telling her stuff, like how maybe it was my fault that my mother had had an accident. "If only I hadn't let her go," I said. "If only I'd never said that the lasagna was too frozen to eat. If only . . . If only . . ."

Gloria held my face in her hands and looked me straight in the eye. "You didn't make your mother go, Hannah. It wasn't to do with you."

And then, as though it was too big for me to hold, I said what I never thought I'd say. "But you don't understand—it wasn't just her going, it was—it was that she'd been drinking. A lot. Like maybe she was drunk."

Gloria put her arm around me and together we rocked back and forth. "I know, I know," she said after a while. "It's been hard on you, hasn't it?"

I nodded against her shoulder.

"There's so much your grandfather and I wanted to do," said Gloria. "And so little we *could* do—except worry about you and your father. And about your mother. But just promise me you'll try to understand something, Hannah. You're not the reason your mother drinks. And you can't keep her from doing it, any more than we can, or even your father."

We sat without saying anything, and then a long time later Gloria stood up. "Now let's see if we can get this room in order. But meanwhile I'm going to call and order a pizza. How about it?"

Fourteen

I didn't think I could ever eat, but I did—a whole half a pizza. We had just finished when Dad called to say that they'd taken Mom to the operating room; that she had internal injuries and a broken ankle and a bunch of cuts and bruises, but they thought she'd be okay.

"What kind of internal injuries?" I asked.

"It's her spleen," said Dad. "She wasn't wearing her seat belt and was thrown against the steering wheel and ruptured her spleen."

I didn't know what a spleen was, but I could tell from the in-a-hurry sound of Dad's voice that this wasn't the time to ask. "How'd it happen? The accident, I mean," I said instead.

"Your mother ran into a bus." And then, after a long silence where I could tell he was trying to decide what to say next, he went on. "The bus was just sitting there and she went through a red light and ran into the back of it. At least, that's what all the witnesses say."

I hung up and told Gloria what Dad had said, but when I asked her what a spleen was, she didn't exactly know either. We had just gotten out the "S" volume of the encyclopedia when Granddad came in. He'd been at a dinner meeting and, when he got home, found Gloria's note telling where she'd gone and about the accident. He asked about Mom and we told him everything we knew and he said that the spleen had something to do with blood but that it couldn't be too important because people lived perfectly well without one. Then he showed me the picture in the encyclopedia, only it turned out to be one of those squishy-looking inside things and I waited just long enough not to seem rude and shut the book. I mean, a spleen may not be all that important but I still didn't like to think of someone taking my mother's *out*.

After that, Gloria said, "Now let's all say a prayer for Katherine, that she'll get well soon and come home quickly." We did, and the thing was that I was really surprised because we're not some super-religious kind of family and probably any other time I'd've thought this was bizarre. Except I liked it. I liked standing there, just the three of us, holding hands, and I especially liked the way, after Gloria had said the prayer part, that

Granddad added, sort of as a reminder to God, "And please help Katherine with her problems."

I knew, by that, he meant the drinking—and I was pretty sure he knew *I* knew. That's all that was said, though, and we dropped hands and turned and started in on the tree mess. And it was done in hardly any time.

"Why don't you go on to bed, Hannah," Gloria said when we'd finished putting the living room back the way it was supposed to be. "We'll be here till your father gets home."

"I can't," I said. "I want to see Dad. I want to hear about Mom. And besides, I haven't done my homework." But I was falling asleep even as I sat there, and after a few minutes I went upstairs. I woke later, when I heard Dad talking to Gloria and Granddad in the downstairs hall, and stumbled out and hung over the banister just long enough to hear Dad say that the operation had gone well before I went back to my room. And back to sleep.

Dad and I both overslept the next morning and we ate breakfast all in a rush and left the house together. "Don't forget," he called after me as I started up the street. "Try and get all your homework done this afternoon—so we can go see your mother tonight."

As soon as I got to school I told Sam about my mother and she went with me to see my teachers so I could explain to them why I hadn't been able to do my homework the night before. The weird thing was that every one of them got really serious and nodded and said how all that ice made the side streets incredibly treacherous. And I just nodded back and never once told any of them that Mom'd been on a perfectly clear main street when she had the accident.

I was working on my homework at the kitchen table when Mom called with a list of things she wanted us to bring to the hospital, stuff like her makeup and a couple of books and her rose-colored robe and her very own slippers so she wouldn't have to wear the paper ones the hospital gave out. Her voice sounded small, and when I asked her about it she said it was from not having her lipstick on and I said it could be from not having her spleen anymore and she said maybe I was right. We both laughed till Mom said it hurt, laughing, I mean, and that she wanted to rest before Dad and I came to visit.

I'd finished my homework by the time Dad got home, and we ate early and set out for the hospital, which kind of gave me the creeps. I mean, I wanted to see Mom and all, I just wanted to see her someplace *else.* I don't like hospitals, and once we got upstairs I followed Dad down the hall without looking right or left even though part of me wanted to see in all those open doors. But the other part of me didn't—in case there might be something gross.

Mom was in the bed by the window and the other bed was empty, which she said was nice, in a way. She looked smaller than she had before the accident and her face was as pale as the lumpy white bandage on her forehead. We pretty much talked about school and the weather and the hospital food, and then about school again. It was almost time for us to leave when Mom shook her head, making a face as if that hadn't been a very good idea, then cleared her throat and said, "You know, that accident was the darnedest thing—the way that bus just pulled in front of me like that."

I stared down at my hands and picked my cuticle and tried not to look at Dad. And I could tell he was trying not to look at me. In fact, we were all the way out of the hospital and in the parking garage before I said, "Does Mom really think that—that the bus pulled out in front of her?"

Dad put his hand on my shoulder for a moment, before he spoke. "She's been told, Hannah. She's been told—even by the police. But I don't know what she thinks."

We went to see Mom the next night and the night after that, and both times, though she said she was glad to see us, I had the feeling that, deep down, she wasn't. Mostly what she did, while we were there, was make little grabbing motions with her hands, as if she was catching lightning bugs or something. And her leg, the one without the cast, kept thrashing under the covers, almost like she was moving around the room. Except she wasn't. Dad asked her if she wanted to get out of bed, only she said no, that she'd been up in a chair a lot during the day and she was tired, and besides that, she was running a fever and nobody knew why. Then she closed her eyes while Dad and I pretty much talked to each other and to the nurse who came to take Mom's blood pressure, till it was time to go home.

On Friday I was in the kitchen trying to make brownies not-from-a-mix and I had to call Mom at the hospital to ask her how to melt the chocolate without it getting all burned and blobby in the bottom of the pan. When she heard my question she started to laugh, like maybe she was never going to stop. And then, sort of hiccuping and catching her breath, she said, "But you've been making brownies since before I was born."

"Mom, it's me, Hannah, and I've only made brownies by myself from a mix and I can't remember how you do it the other way. About the chocolate, I mean."

"Hannah? Hannah?" said Mom.

"Yes, me," I said.

"Hannah," said Mom again, and then her voice sort of fell apart, as if any minute she was going to cry. "Oh, Hannah, I thought you were my *mother*. Do you know, she hasn't called me the whole time I've been in this hospital, or come to see me either—and it's been days now."

"Your mother?" I said. Then I felt myself go cold and hot and cold again because I knew that my mother's mother, who would've been my grandmother, had been dead since before I was born.

"Hannah," said Mom from the other end of the phone. "Hannah, maybe you could call her for me. Maybe she doesn't know I'm here. Maybe she doesn't know the number."

"Yeah, well, Mom, maybe," I said because I couldn't think what else to say. I mean, if *my* mother thinks *her* mother is still alive, how can *I* be the one to tell her she's not?

After I hung up I called Gloria and she told me to look for Mom's double boiler and to put water in the bottom and the chocolate in the top. Except by the time

I hung up from her just the thought of brownies made me feel sick and I closed the cookbook and sat there staring at it until Dad got home.

"It's got to be the medicine, something she's taking. Sometimes there're strange side effects," said Dad when I told him about what Mom had said. "We'll see if she's better tonight."

But she wasn't. When we walked into Mom's room it looked like a tornado had hit it. Or maybe she was the tornado. She was rocking from side to side, kicking out with her legs, even the one with the cast on it, and holding her arms overhead. "What're you doing here?" she said, getting suddenly still.

"Visiting you," said Dad.

"How'd you get here?" said Mom.

"Drove," I said.

"All the way?" said Mom. "From Baltimore?"

"This *is* Baltimore," I said, before I could think not to.

But Mom just churned the air with her hand, as if she was clearing smoke away. She caught hold of the sleeve of my ski coat and pulled me close, saying, "And why'd you wear this heavy jacket? You won't need anything like this in Florida."

I opened my mouth and closed it again. I looked at Dad.

"Well, you never know," he said. "And the weather's so changeable it doesn't hurt to be prepared."

Mom pushed herself up against the slanty part of the bed and looked at him, like maybe it was a trick answer. "Where're you staying?" she said quickly. "What hotel?"

And then all I knew was that I had to get out of that room. I faked a cough and mumbled something about a drink of water and turned and left. I sat in the lounge by the elevators and watched people come and go and pretended I was there to visit someone else. I stayed put for a long time, till Dad came and beckoned me. "Come and say good night," he said.

I didn't want to go in my mother's room, but I did, and when I bent to kiss her good night she pushed me away and looked over my shoulder, as if there was something there that neither Dad nor I could see.

"They'll run some tests," my father said when we were in the elevator. "I talked to the doctor and they'll run some tests."

When we got home there was a message on the answering machine from Aunt Pauli, who wanted to know why Mom had telephoned and said that she was calling from a hospital in Florida, when she was actually right in Baltimore. And would someone please call and explain to her what was going on.

Dad went to visit Mom by himself on Saturday and when he got home he headed for the phone. I started in from the sun porch to see him but all of a sudden I could tell by the way he was talking, all hushed and low, that he didn't want me to hear. And I knew it had to do with Mom. I sort of froze, not moving from where I was, and then tiptoed the rest of the way into the dining room, sliding onto a chair and hoping that, maybe, if he saw me, he'd think I'd been there all along and wasn't really eavesdropping.

"Yeah, Dad, it's DT's," I heard him say and I knew that he was talking to Granddad. "Apparently, it's her system reacting to not having any alcohol since she's been in the hospital, at having to go cold turkey. At least, they're just about sure that's what it is."

There was a pause and I knew that was Granddad talking and then my father went on. "Yes, yes. Probably." Another pause, then, "I'll keep you posted. Goodbye, now."

"What's DT's?" I said, jumping up and going into the kitchen, suddenly not caring whether Dad knew I'd been listening or not. "You were talking about Mom, I could tell, and what's *DT's*?"

"Oh, Hannah," said Dad. He was standing with his hand still on the phone, and his face was gray and ragged-looking.

"She's *my* mother and I want to *know*," I said. "What *is* it?"

Dad reached for the kettle, filled it, and took it back to the stove. He shook instant coffee into a mug and added sugar. And all the while I could tell from the way he was looking at me and not looking at me that he didn't want to tell.

"What *is* it?" I said again.

"It's . . . well . . . it comes from . . . it means delirium tremens, and in your mother's case it's a withdrawal . . ."

"A withdrawal from what?" I said.

"From alcohol. Because she hasn't had any alcohol since she's been in the hospital."

"But that's *good*, isn't it?" I said. "I mean, we want for Mom not to drink."

"Yes," said Dad, pouring hot water into his mug and taking it over to the table, nodding for me to sit across from him. "But the thing is that it's been a shock to her system and her body's reacting. That accounts for the way she's been behaving, the way she's been talking." He picked up his mug and put it down again, shaking his head. "She didn't know me today."

"But can't they do something? It's a hospital," I said.

"It's not that simple," said Dad. "I mean, they could give her a drink—something alcoholic—and bring her out of it that way, but then we'd be back where we started and I can't agree to that. And the doctors are being very cautious about using medicine to help her over this until they make sure that hitting her head in the accident is not to blame. They're going to do another CAT scan."

"But what'll happen—if it is what you said? If it is DT's?"

"It will gradually wear away and your mother'll get better. From this, anyway."

"But will she drink again?" I asked.

"Maybe, probably, unless she . . . unless we can find a way to . . ." And my father turned aside, but not before I could see the tears in his eyes.

He stood at the sink, washing his mug, filling it with water and emptying it, filling it and emptying it.

"Anyway," he said, after a while, "the doctors and I think it would be better if you didn't see your mother until she's her old self again."

I need to see Mom, I wanted to shout, but when I looked at Dad his face was even grayer than it'd been before and I bit my lip and didn't say anything. Except inside my head where the words kept spinning all night long. *I need to see Mom. I need to see Mom.*

The next day, after lunch, Dad settled down at the dining room table with a bunch of papers, saying that he had to get them corrected before he did another thing, that he would go to visit Mom that night. I wandered around the house, stopping to rearrange the dolls in the dollhouse, turning on the TV, then turning it off again, looking at the comics in the Sunday paper. Then I grabbed my camera and put on my coat, telling Dad that I was going to get Sam so we could take some pictures. And the thing was that I think I really meant it—when I said it. But maybe not, because why else did I take a bunch of money out of my wallet and shove it into my jeans pocket before I left the house?

Anyway, I took the bus to the hospital and went up the stairs, all the way to the fifth floor, figuring that maybe the nurses wouldn't see me if I didn't come walking out of the elevator right in front of them. There was a sign on Mom's door that said NO VISITORS and for a minute I stopped.

"But I'm a daughter, not a visitor," I said under my breath, looking down the hall to make sure nobody was coming after me. Then I pushed the door open and went into my mother's room. The shades were drawn and everything was in shadows. Mom lay without moving and the sides were up on the bed, like maybe it was a crib or something. And the worst part: her arms and legs were tied to the rails, so she couldn't go anywhere even if she'd wanted to. Her hair was tangled and her face was small and sunken-looking and for a minute I wasn't really sure if that person there in front of me *was* my mother. Except that Mom's books were on the bedside table, her rose-colored robe was on the chair, and the pink-and-white flowers Dad and I'd brought on Friday night were wilting on the windowsill.

I moved closer to the bed, feeling sad and scared and shaky on the inside. And then suddenly a great huge anger took hold of me and filled me all the way to the top. I mean, I was angry at the hospital for tying her like that and at my dad for telling me not to come and at myself for coming. And most of all I was angry at my mother: for drinking and driving and having the accident; for thinking she was in Florida when she wasn't, and getting so she *had* to be tied.

I wanted to *do* something, to yell and scream and get back at her. And then, without thinking about it, I took my camera out of my pocket and started taking pictures as fast as I could. Of her with her mouth open and with the ties on her arms and legs. Of her looking at me and not seeing me. Snap. Snap. Snap. And the flash lit the corners of the room.

The door flew open and a nurse was there. "What's going on here?" she asked.

I pushed past her and ran along the hall and down the steps, through the lobby to the cold icy outside air. And, without even waiting for the bus, I started to walk, all the way home.

Fifteen

Dad was still sitting at the dining room table when I got home, sort of mumbling under his breath and shaking his head the way he does when he corrects papers. Especially when they're not as good as he thinks they ought to be. "You and Sam have fun?" he said, looking up, then down again.

"Hmmmmuhh," I said and went on to the kitchen to get something to eat because that's pretty much what I always do when I come into the house. But this time I wasn't hungry. I took a handful of pretzels, anyway, and carried them up to my room and dropped them, along with my camera, onto the bed. I kicked off my shoes and wiggled my toes and wondered if they'd ever be warm again. I stood by the window for a while, looking out at the back yard, and when the phone rang I let it ring.

After a few minutes Dad knocked on the door and came in. "That was one of the nurses from the hospital on the phone," he said. "She told me that you were there, that you were pretty upset when you left, and that she's been worrying about you ever since and finally decided she'd better call."

"I *had* to go," I said. "I had to see what was wrong with Mom, only now I wish I hadn't." I went to the window and stood looking out again. I heard him settle onto the desk chair.

"I wish I hadn't ever seen her like that—why does she *do* it? Why does she let herself *get* that way? Why?"

"I wish you hadn't seen her that way either, Hannah. I wanted to spare you that." He stopped, and for a minute I thought he wasn't going to say any more. Then he sighed and went on. "I'm afraid the time's come when we're going to have to accept it straight out: your mother is an alcoholic."

"No," I said, turning to him. "Don't call her that." And then all of a sudden I remembered phoning the HELPline and going to the library to find books that'd tell me what was wrong with Mom. Only here was Dad saying it out loud: what we both had known and didn't want to know.

"Don't call her that," I said again.

He held out his hand and I went to sit on the foot of

the bed, across from him. "It's not a pretty word," he said, "but it's the truth and something I haven't really faced up to."

"But she can't be," I said, digging my toes into the rug until they hurt. "I mean, maybe sometimes she drinks too much, but *real* alcoholics are bums. They're people in bars and sleeping in doorways and in the station, like that one we saw the time we went to Philadelphia on the train."

"They're other people, too. Everyday kinds of people —doctors and teachers, painters and plumbers. And they all have a disease called alcoholism."

I thought for a minute before I said, "Miss Duncan talked about that in health class but—I don't know—I had trouble understanding it or even believing it. What kind of disease is it? What's it do?"

"Just what we've been seeing," my father said.

"Make her, you know, drunk? Make her fall down and drive into buses and say things and then not remember that she said them?"

"It makes her not able to control her use of alcohol because of something in her body that means she reacts to it differently, from, say, the way I do. Or Granddad or Gloria or Mr. Porter next door."

"If it's a disease, then why don't they cure her, give her some medicine or a shot or an operation or something?"

"It's not that easy," said Dad, getting up and moving around the room before coming back to sit on the other bed. "There *isn't* any medicine or shot or operation to cure your mother—"

I started to say something, but he put his hand up. "Her disease can be stopped so she'll be able to lead a normal life—without any drinking."

"Let's do that, then," I said.

"We can't," said Dad.

"Why can't we?"

"Because I think it's finally gotten through to me that first your mother has to decide on her own that *she's* ready to stop. That *she* needs help."

The phone rang then and Dad went to answer it. He came back to say that Gloria wanted us to come over for potluck supper and afterward I could wait there while he went to see Mom.

"Let's get ready, shall we?" he said. "We'll talk some more later on."

After Dad went downstairs I turned and saw my camera still on my bed where I'd dropped it. I picked it up and held it for a minute, thinking about what Dad had said, the part about Mom having a disease, and how she had to be the one to want to make it go away. Then I took out the film and sat it on the corner of my dresser before heading into the bathroom to wash my face.

For the next few days Dad went to see Mom by himself and afterward, when he got home, he'd tell me how she was doing. It was weird and kind of scary, the way it sounded as if she was coming back from a faraway trip that she'd taken on her own. She wasn't tied to the bed anymore, she knew my father, she didn't see things that nobody else could see or think she was in Florida.

And then one day, when he came in from work, he

said, "Your mother called me at school today to say she wants to see you, Hannah. So we can go after supper, if you've gotten most of your homework done."

I guess Dad must've known how the thoughts were going off in my head like firecrackers. All about how I didn't want to go to the hospital again, and what would it be like seeing Mom, after the way she was the last time I saw her. Anyway, he looked up right in the middle of making hamburgers and said, "It'll be okay, Hannah. It'll be okay." And then, once we got there, he kept his hand under my elbow all the way to her room.

Mom was sitting on a chair, wearing her rose-colored robe that was now too big for her. She had a walking cast on one leg, and her face was pale and sort of caved in, and when I leaned over to kiss her she caught hold of my hand, like maybe she was never going to let it go.

"Somebody fixed your hair," I said, reaching out with my other hand.

"I did it," said Mom. "I hobbled into the bathroom and stuck my head in the sink." She let go of my hand and pushed herself up out of the chair. "Come on, let's go out in the hall and I'll show you how I can navigate."

I pulled away from her and went to stand by the window, pretending to look at the cards lined along the sill. I mean, there was no way I was going out in that hall with my mother and have all those people look at me and think there goes the daughter of *that woman*. The one who had DT's and thought she was in Florida instead of Maryland and caught at lightning bugs when there weren't any there. Then I felt ashamed of being ashamed. But I still wasn't going.

"Please," said Mom. She had hold of Dad with one hand and was kind of reaching out to me with the other.

"We need you, Hannah," my father said.

I couldn't not go, after that, so I took my place on Mom's other side and the three of us squeezed our way through the door and out into the hall, where we walked the whole entire fifth floor. And the awesome thing was that whenever we passed people, even at the nurses' station, they all just smiled and spoke to Mom like maybe she had appendicitis or a virus or something.

The *good* news was that Mom was scheduled to come home on Saturday. Except that from the way Dad looked when he didn't know I was watching, anybody'd think it was really *bad* news.

"Don't you want Mom to come home?" I asked after we'd left the hospital on Friday night.

"Want your mother to come home?" he said in one of those fake cheery voices people use when they're trying to sell something. "You bet I do." Then he beeped a gross kind of tune with the horn, which is something I can positively swear my father'd never done before.

Later that night, when I'd finished the book I was reading and wasn't quite sleepy, I went downstairs. Dad was in the sun porch, staring at the TV, holding the remote control and not even channel-surfing, which let me know that something was definitely wrong.

"Are you thinking about Mom?" I asked, sitting on one end of the couch and pulling my legs up under me.

"Your mother?" he said, starting in with that fake

voice again. Then he stopped, and in the funky light from the TV it was as if I could see my father's face sort of crumble. "I'm worried about her," he said.

"But she's not drinking," I said.

"No, but the doctor called me at school today. He said he'd had a long talk with your mother today, that he'd spelled it all out: about the DT's and the drunk driving charge and how she'd be required to go into some kind of treatment program because of it."

"What'd Mom say?"

"She tried to brush it off and just kept saying that she wanted to go home. That she was okay—that she'd *be* okay." He flipped through three channels of news before turning off the set and saying into the sudden dark, "It's as if none of what's happened is real to her yet. None of it."

We picked Mom up at the hospital the next day and it was kind of spooky. I mean, the weekend was suddenly a trillion hours long and we all moved carefully, as if maybe we didn't really know each other very well. And for once, when Monday morning came, I was glad to get out of there and go to school.

I thought Dad and I'd done a pretty good job of housekeeping while Mom was in the hospital, until I got home Monday afternoon and saw everything all neat and dusted and kind of comfortable. The way Mom makes a place look. There was a bakery bag on the kitchen table, so I figured somebody'd stopped by, and I was just reaching in, hoping for an oatmeal raisin cookie, when all of a sudden I knew the house was *too* quiet.

"Mom," I said. "Mom?"

I opened the cellar door, but it was dark down there. I went through the first floor and up the stairs, stopping outside of my mother's room, then tiptoeing the rest of the way. Mom was huddled in the bed with the covers pulled up over her head, like maybe she was hiding from something.

She's been drinking, I thought. She's been drinking and she's drunk and things'll be the way they were before. I remembered what Dad said about how Mom had a disease, only the more I tried to think, the more the idea seemed to slide away from me. "She's *sick*," I told myself, looking at the hunched-up shape that was my mother. "She's *drunk*," I answered back. And the words fought inside my head.

I checked the bedside table, the dresser, the floor, for a bottle, a glass. I hurried into the bathroom, rooting through the linen closet, the dirty clothes hamper. I ran downstairs, opening cupboards in the kitchen, pulling things out of the hall closet. I looked under furniture and behind books in the bookcases before racing on to the cellar. I searched the dark room and the laundry room and even the cobwebby places in back of the furnace. I went outside and dug through the trash.

By the time I got to the second floor again, I was gasping and out of breath. "Mom?" I said, moving around to the far side of the bed.

The pictures were spilled there, all over the floor. I leaned over to pick them up, putting them in a stack in the palm of my hand, flipping through them. And then one of those creepy feelings came over me—the kind where you feel like what's happening now has already happened sometime in the past. I went through the pictures again, looking down at my mother in her hospital bed, at the ties on her arms and legs, at her face sunk in the pillow, her eyes staring at nothing.

There was a whimpering noise from under the blanket and my mother crawled out. She was fully dressed, with even a shoe on her good foot, and she sat on the edge of the bed holding tight to the pillow she'd pulled over onto her lap.

"I haven't had a drink," she said, in a voice I could hardly hear. Then she put out her hand, reaching for the pictures.

"Mom, no," I said, stepping back. "Where'd you—how'd you—I never meant for you to—"

She drew her hand back and held it with her other one. "I was restless this morning, after I'd straightened up a bit, looking for something to do. And I found the film on your dresser and thought I'd develop it for you, as a surprise." She reached out again.

"Mom—please—"

"Let me look." And her voice was suddenly strong. "I have to know."

I heard my father come in the front door, heard him come up the steps, saw him standing in the doorway. I handed the pictures to my mother and watched as she looked at them.

"Is this what it was like—what I was like?" she asked.

I thought I was about to choke on all the words piled up inside of me. After a very long time I shook my head no, and said, "Yes."

"Is *this* what I looked like?" she said, holding up another. "And *this*?"

I didn't say anything and Mom went on. "It must've been pretty bad for you—for you and your father."

"Pretty bad," I said.

She pushed the pictures onto the floor and dug her fists into the pillow. "When I saw these, when I printed them up this afternoon and *really* saw them, it was worse than anything that's ever happened to me— worse than the accident and the police and what I knew I was doing to myself. I was so scared about—I was scared thinking about losing you and your father. Because of me—what all I'd done." She shook her head slowly from side to side.

Dad and I piled onto the bed next to her, but she sort of pushed us away. "No, first let me—I have to— The doctor in the hospital tried to tell me, but I didn't—it was as if I was almost—but couldn't—" She twisted one corner of the pillow and her voice, when she spoke, sounded like breaking glass. "I'm an alcoholic and I've got to do something. Got to get some help."

And we all just sat there listening to each other breathe. I wanted to touch Mom, to take hold of her, the way I knew Dad wanted to, but it was as if we couldn't yet. As if this wasn't the time.

My mother felt around under the covers, pulling out a piece of paper and holding it up so I could read the letters AA, and a phone number. "The doctor gave me this before I left the hospital—in case I ever—for when I— And I want the two of you here with me when I call."

Her hands were shaking when she punched in the numbers, but her voice, when she spoke, was steady. And I heard, as if from far away, my mother asking for someone to come, saying that she hadn't had a drink but that she wanted one and wanted not to take it. That she needed help.

Then we were all on the bed together, holding on to one another.

Afterward we went downstairs and sat at the kitchen table and ate cookies out of the bakery bag, and waited. And when the doorbell rang and Mom got up to go and answer it, the look on her face was happy and sad, and mostly scared.

Sixteen

Helen was one of the two people who came to the house that time way back in January when Mom called the AA number, which I found out later was for Alcoholics Anonymous. She became Mom's sponsor and took her to her first meeting that very night, where she met a bunch of other alcoholics who all work at helping themselves—and helping each other. Ever since then Helen and Mom've gotten to be friends and talked a lot and gone to about a million more meetings. They've even told each other things about themselves, which they didn't have to do because that's the thing about AA—you can stay anonymous, if that's the way you want it. And the awesome part is that in that whole long almost-five-months time my mother hasn't had a drink.

It's weird, but those five months seem to have stretched out forever. Mostly, I guess, because of the way Mom always talks about taking them one day at a time. That's one of the things they teach you in AA— how you only have to think about today.

"A person can certainly go without a drink for a day, right?" Mom says over and over.

"Right," Dad and I always answer her, as loud as we can.

That's why seeing Helen's car parked out front when I got home from school today freaked me out. Why it gave me a creepy feeling, like something was about to happen—or maybe already had. It's not that I don't like her, because I do, it's just that I know she's a travel agent in a downtown office and I'm not used to seeing her here in the middle of a Thursday afternoon. Anyway, I took a deep breath, opened the door, and went inside, and right away I heard voices coming from the kitchen.

"Hannah, is that you?" Mom called. "Come on back."

She and Helen were sitting there drinking coffee, which was okay, and normal, except that in the middle of the table, between them, was a bottle of vodka. And that bottle seemed larger than the stove and the refrigerator and the whole entire kitchen. I tried not to look at it all the while Mom was telling me to get a snack and Helen was asking about school. I tried not to look at it as I was taking a Coke from under the sink and getting ice and opening a new bag of pretzels. I tried not to look at it—but I did.

"I didn't *drink* it," Mom said, reaching out and running her fingers over the unbroken seal at the top of the bottle. "I didn't drink it."

I stood there for what seemed like forever, not knowing what to say.

"I didn't drink it," Mom said again.

"That's good," I finally said, my voice sounding small and croaky. "That's really good, Mom." I sat on the chair she pushed out for me and drank a couple of quick gulps of Coke so that the bubbles prickled up the back of my nose.

"But I *wanted* to," Mom went on. She moved the bottle over in front of me so I couldn't *not* see it. "I wanted to, but I didn't."

I guess they could tell I didn't know what to say again because Helen touched me on the arm and said, "Is there something you want to ask your mom, Hannah?" Which I thought was pretty dumb because if I'd had anything to say I would've said it. Except that all of a sudden I heard my same croaky voice saying, "How come?"

"How come I didn't drink it?" said Mom. "Because after I went out and bought it and brought it home and was sitting here at the table looking at it, I knew, somehow, that I wanted *not* to drink it, even more than I wanted *to* drink it. That's when I called Helen and asked her to come."

"I mean, how come you wanted it in the first place?" I said.

"I don't know," said Mom. "Maybe I was scared."

"Scared?" I said.

"Helen and I've been talking about it."

"Yes," said Helen, "and I've been telling your mother that people sometimes have setbacks. She knows that from the—"

"Scared?" I said again, not caring that I was interrupting. I pushed the bottle aside so I could see my mother, who looked really together, and not as if she was afraid of anything. "Scared of what?"

"I guess of the opening of the show this evening. In just a couple of hours, in fact," she said, looking up at the clock.

"But, Mom, it's what you've been waiting for—a show of your own, in a gallery downtown." I turned to Helen and said, "Do you know about it? Did she tell you?" And before she had a chance to answer I went rattling on. "Did she tell you how this woman who owns a gallery saw one of her pictures on a wall of a friend's house—it was of a really cool swing hanging from a branch of this humongous tree—in black-and-white and all filled with shadows and sunlight both at the same time. Anyway, she, the lady, called Mom up and asked if she had any more and Mom took a bunch down and the lady *loved* them and offered her a show and it starts today, with a reception and everything. And how practically all spring Mom's been taking more pictures—not weddings but the *real* ones, the kind she likes—so she could pick the best."

I caught my breath and kept on going. "And how she and Dad've been matting them, and framing them, and how the other night we all three went down and hung them. And are you going?" I finished up, holding the bag of pretzels out to Helen.

"I wouldn't miss it," she said. "But, Hannah, don't you see, with all that, how your mother could be just a little bit scared?"

"I guess," I said after a while. And even though Mom'd said it before, I wasn't sure, till that very moment, that I'd ever actually *believed* that grownups could get *really* scared.

"What if all those people I've invited actually come?" Mom said.

I thought of the names Mom'd let me add to her invitation list and said, "Mine will. At least, most of them, anyway. Sam and her mother and father and Mr. Jones, my homeroom teacher, and maybe Rosa, if her mother gets home from work in time, except not Effie, because she was out sick today."

"And what if they all hate my work?" Mom said.

"And what if they all *love* it and buy everything up and you become really famous like Ansel Adams or Joel Meyerowitz or one of those other photographers you sometimes talk about? What if that?" I said.

Mom and Helen both laughed and after a while I did, too. Then Helen stood up and said she'd run along so we could shower and get dressed before Dad came home, and that she'd see us at the gallery. Except that she didn't actually leave but just sort of stood there, as if she was waiting for something.

"What about *that*?" I said, pointing to the bottle of vodka.

"Oh, yes," said Mom. She started to get up and then

stopped and sat down again. "What should I do with it?" She raised her eyebrows and looked at Helen.

"What do you think you should do with it?" she said.

Mom waited for what seemed like ages without saying anything. Then she grabbed the bottle and twisted the cap off.

My heart pounded and my hands were clammy-cold. What if she *drinks* it, I thought. What if . . .

Mom got up and went over to the sink and held the bottle upside down. With her other hand she clung to the edge of the counter, like maybe the floor wasn't steady beneath her. But she kept on pouring.

We got to the gallery early, before the reception even began, and it was really impressive, with the room all hushed and about a trillion lights coming out of the ceiling and Mom's pictures sort of wrapping around us. I mean, I'd seen them all at home, and there, too, on the night we hung the show. But tonight they seemed different, both new and familiar at the same time. There was a table set up in an alcove where a girl with green hair was serving wine and Perrier. We each took a glass, and right away Mom started tearing at the edges of her paper napkin and saying, "What if nobody comes?"

She was just starting on her second Perrier (and her second napkin) when the gallery lady came swooping in, apologizing for not being there to greet us and saying that she'd been back in her office tied up with a long-distance call she couldn't cut short. She and Mom started talking business, Dad drifted off to talk to the Porters, who'd just come in, and I headed for the baskets of peanuts and raw vegetables set out on the bar. Next time I turned around, the room was swirling with people.

I saw Gloria and Granddad, Aunt Pauli, Uncle Bill, and even Casey. I saw Sam, and Mr. and Mrs. Sardo, Rosa and her mother, and Mr. Jones, from school, who looked at each picture close up, then stood back and looked at it again before moving on. I saw a bunch of Mom and Dad's friends and the new neighbors from down the street and, way at the far end of the gallery, Helen looking at the picture of the swing I'd told her about. And I saw about a ton of people I'd never seen before.

Later, when the crowd had thinned out, Sam and I were standing there while her parents and Mr. Jones talked to Mom and Dad. After a bit, Granddad and Gloria joined us, and, when he got a chance, Granddad said, "It seems a shame to end this celebration now. Why don't we continue it at Uncle Lee's, over dinner."

Mr. and Mrs. Sardo said they had to get home and Mr. Jones said he had to go think up something to do for the last few days of school. Dad told Sam's parents that he'd drop her off after dinner, and Gloria was just looking around for Aunt Pauli and Uncle Bill and Casey, to see if they wanted to come with us, when Mom said, "I'm sorry, Dad. That sounds great, but I'm afraid I can't make it. I have to go to my AA meeting now."

Right then I wanted the floor under where I was standing to open up and me to disappear forever. I mean, I couldn't believe my mother had said that. Out loud, for everyone to hear.

There was a sudden silence all around us, so that for the first time I could hear the sound of traffic out on the street. And after what seemed like ages everybody started to talk again—but I still wanted the floor to open up. I still wished Mom hadn't said it. The next thing I knew, Granddad had me and Sam each by an arm, saying, "Let's take one last tour of this wonderful show before we leave for dinner, shall we?"

The three of us walked along, taking our time and looking at the pictures again. Granddad kept talking, all about light and shadow and focus and stuff, pointing out things to Sam, asking her questions. And the whole time I was thinking about Mom: how I was really, really glad she wasn't drinking anymore but how I sometimes wished she didn't have to go to so many AA meetings. Or talk about them.

We stopped in front of one of the few pictures of people in the show. It was of a witch and a fairy princess Mom had taken one Halloween. I remembered how she'd run to get her camera and had the kids go down and start up the porch steps again, holding out gigantic trick-or-treat bags.

"Do you think maybe someday your mother'd take a picture of the two of us, Hannah?" Sam asked. "A big one, like this, so we'd have it for when we're grownup and you're a writer and I'm a veterinarian and we have children of our own and probably won't live down the street from each other."

Then I felt as if I was taking this giant leap out into space and I said something I didn't know I was going to say, except I'm pretty sure I'd been thinking about it, somewhere down inside of me. And having Granddad there, still holding on to my arm, made it seem okay. Anyway, I said, "Yeah, sure, I bet she will, but let's wait till you come to the beach with us this summer and she can take it in this cove I like, where the light's really awesome. Okay?"

Seventeen

The beginning of the summer was long and a little bit boring, the way summers mostly are. I went to the library a lot and read about a mountain of books, even some that were on my school reading list. I hung out with Sam and Rosa and Effie, except when one or the other of them was on vacation, and we ate a lot of pizza and frozen yogurt and kept our fingers crossed that we'd meet some boys who were older than eighth grade, and mysterious. I worked with Mom in the darkroom and learned to develop my own film. And I had a sort-of job, baby-sitting for Mrs. Carolli across the street. The trouble with that was she only sort-of paid me.

The way it worked was that Mrs. Carolli asked me if I'd like to go to the pool with her and watch her kids some and that she'd pay me for it. The kids, Sally and Jimbo, were three years and eighteen months and spent all their time trying to drown each other in the baby pool and I spent all my time trying to stop them while Mrs. Carolli sat in the shade playing cards with her friends and drinking diet Coke. And when it came time to pay me she gave me hardly anything at all. I guess, probably, because I was supposed to be having such a great time, which I wasn't. When I complained to Mom she said to use it as a "learning experience" and next time to make sure I had the business details worked out in advance. Which didn't help for *this* time, and besides I was sure the baby pool was filled with baby pee, which, if you ask me, is pretty disgusting.

Anyway, from the middle of July to the end of the month I started counting the days till we went to the beach and my sort-of job ended. And when Mrs. Carolli asked if I wanted to help with the kids a couple of times a week after school in the fall, so she could go jogging, I said I'd have to wait and see how much homework I had. I probably will, though, especially since she said she'd have to start paying me what she paid her other baby-sitters *now that she'd trained me*. And I didn't even laugh.

Mom and Dad and I came to the beach at the beginning of August and the first thing I did is what I always do—just walk around and remember the place. Except for new yellow dishes in the cupboard, everything was exactly the same and I hurried and unpacked. By the time I finished, Mandy, Sue, and Jessie Lee were at the door yelling for me to come out. I couldn't wait to tell them how Sam was coming down for the last week of vacation, and on the first rainy day the four of us wrote her one big long letter telling her what we were doing and what she should bring and all that.

What we were doing was what we pretty much do every summer: going to the beach in Ocean City and out in Mandy's father's boat, crabbing in the bay, eating Granddad's blueberry pancakes, playing Monopoly, and moonbathing. We spent even more time at the pool this year because the funny thing was that last year's nerds weren't anywhere near as nerdy as they'd been before, and one of them, named Will, even taught me to do a back dive.

Sam came from Baltimore by bus and Mom and I met her in Ocean City. While we were waiting out in front of the terminal for the bus to come in I suddenly got scared, with that sort-of-looking-over-my-shoulder feeling I'd had ever since Mom'd stopped drinking, wondering if things'd keep being okay. I didn't have time to worry for long because just as I was settling down to it the bus pulled onto the parking lot and there was Sam, banging on the window and waving at us.

When we got back to the house, Mandy and Sue and Jessie Lee were waiting for us. The first hour we spent showing Sam around and after that it was as though she'd been there forever, or as long as we had. All week we pretty much did the usual stuff except that once Jessie Lee's mother let us all have a sleepover on their living room floor and once Dad and Mom took Sam and me into Ocean City, to the Crab House, for dinner. *And*, one morning when the light was really awesome,

Mom took pictures of Sam and me, down in the cove I like a lot.

My birthday was on the twenty-ninth and we had the party at Gloria and Granddad's, same as we always do. It was kind of different, though, because this year we had to wait to get started till later than usual so Mom'd have time to go into town to an AA meeting. And my cousin Casey brought a girl named Libby, which was weird, but nice. While we were waiting for Mom to get home, Gloria gave out some sparklers she'd gotten from someplace and Dad lit them for us and we tried to write our names in the air with them before they went out.

Afterward Casey and Libby headed off to a beach party, the grownups played Pictionary, and Mandy, Sue, Jessie Lee, Sam, and I went down on the pier and moonbathed. We stayed there till it was really late and there were nothing but night sounds all around us.

"Does your mother always go to so many AA meetings?" Sam asked from her bed on the other side of the room later that night.

"Yeah, I guess," I said. And then, because it was dark and having Sam there seemed so comfortable, I went on. "She goes to just about one a day and sometimes I—well, sometimes it's a pain and I asked her once why she had to go so much and she said it's because she *needs* to and maybe later she won't have to go to so many, but maybe she will."

"What's it like—with your mother and all?" Sam said after a long time and her voice sounded sleepy and faraway.

I waited awhile till her breathing was deep and slow

and I could tell she was asleep. I whispered her question over to myself and thought about how I'd answer it.

"What's it like—with your mother and all?"

Better than it was before, about a zillion times better. And then I thought how I still don't always understand about alcoholism being a disease and how I sometimes get mad and don't see why Mom can't say right out that she'll never drink again and how she just says over and over that she'll take one day at a time. I thought about how I still have the feeling of waiting for something to happen and will it ever go away and how maybe in the fall I'll go to an Alateen meeting, which is for kids of alcoholics and where you get to talk about what's happening in your life. And I thought how maybe I'll tell this to Sam sometime when she's awake.

And I thought about the things I know I'll never tell her: about how when Mom went away we didn't *really* know where she was, about how she ran into the bus, and, more than anything, how she had DT's. I'll never, never, never tell that.

I got up early the next morning and tiptoed into the bathroom to get dressed so I wouldn't wake Sam. When I went outside, the Hannah column was taped to the door, the way I knew it would be, and I sat down on the step to read it.

"Hannah at Thirteen" it said across the top. "My granddaughter, Hannah, is thirteen," Granddad had written. Then he talked about a lot of things that happened during the year, like my being a gypsy dancer at school and getting a camera and learning to develop my own pictures; about my friends at home and at the beach, too.

Then there was another part that I read really fast because I was afraid to see what it said—and then went back and read slowly again, because it was okay. That was where he wrote about the year in between twelve and thirteen being a real growing-up year for me and how I'd come through some difficult times with flying colors and that he was proud of me. It was all stuff *I* knew had to do with what'd happened with Mom, but that nobody just reading it would know. And by the time I got to the bottom line where he said, "Happy birthday, Hannah," my eyes were all blurry with tears.

After a while I got up and went inside and put the Hannah column under the ladybug magnet on the refrigerator door so nothing would happen to it. Then I went out again and along the road to Granddad's house. He was sitting on the porch, reading the paper, when I got there.

"Morning, Hannah," he said.

"Morning, Granddad." I sat on the steps and concentrated on making patterns in the pine needles on the path with my bare feet. "I read your column—the one, you know . . . Well, thanks."

He leaned down and gave me a sort-of hug, because he's not really a hugging person. "And I meant every word," he said. "I *am* proud of you, Hannah."

My eyes were blurry again and I blinked and stared hard at my big toe.

Granddad cleared his throat a couple of times before

he said, "So, what do you have planned for your next-to-last day of vacation?"

"Today? Today we're going over to Assateague Island, for swimming and a picnic. Mom, Dad, Sam, and I. You guys want to come?"

"Well, we would if we could, but Gloria and I're going up to Rehoboth to meet friends for lunch. But I tell you, why don't you run over and get your friend Sam and we'll all have blueberry pancakes, to start the day."

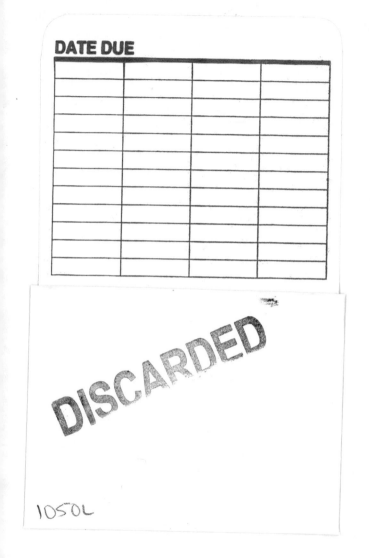

DATE DUE

1050L